Other books by J. D. Salinger

THE CATCHER IN THE RYE

FRANNY AND ZOOEY

RAISE HIGH THE ROOF BEAM, CARPENTERS and
SEYMOUR: AN INTRODUCTION

J. D. SALINGER
NINE STORIES

BANTAM BOOKS
TORONTO · NEW YORK · LONDON · SYDNEY

RL 7, IL 9+

NINE STORIES

*A Bantam Book / published by arrangement with
Little, Brown and Company, Inc.*

PRINTING HISTORY

*Little, Brown edition published April 1953
17 printings through July 1965*

Modern Library edition published October 1959

*Bantam edition / October 1964
25 printngs through August 1981*

ACKNOWLEDGMENTS

*Of the nine stories in the book the following seven appeared
originally in* THE NEW YORKER: *"A Perfect Day for Bananafish,"
"Uncle Wiggily in Connecticut," "Just Before the War with the
Eskimos," "The Laughing Man," "For Esme—with Love and
Squalor," "Pretty Mouth and Green My Eyes," and "Teddy."
The author is grateful to* THE NEW YORKER *for permission to
reprint.*

The author also wishes to thank HARPER'S MAGAZINE *for permission to reprint "Down at the Dinghy."*

ISBN 0-553-20512-9

Published simultaneously in the United States and Canada

PRINTED IN THE UNITED STATES OF AMERICA

34 33 32 31 30 29 28 27 26

To
DOROTHY OLDING
and
GUS LOBRANO

We know the sound of two hands clapping.
But what is the sound of one hand clapping?

—A ZEN KOAN

Contents

Nine Stories

A Perfect Day for Bananafish

THERE WERE ninety-seven New York advertising men in the hotel, and, the way they were monopolizing the long-distance lines, the girl in 507 had to wait from noon till almost two-thirty to get her call through. She used the time, though. She read an article in a women's pocket-size magazine, called "Sex Is Fun—or Hell." She washed her comb and brush. She took the spot out of the skirt of her beige suit. She moved the button on her Saks blouse. She tweezed out two freshly surfaced hairs in her mole. When the operator finally rang her room, she was sitting on the window seat and had almost finished putting lacquer on the nails of her left hand.

She was a girl who for a ringing phone dropped exactly nothing. She looked as if her phone had been ringing continually ever since she had reached puberty.

With her little lacquer brush, while the phone was ringing, she went over the nail of her little finger, accentuating the line of the moon. She then replaced the cap on the bottle of lacquer and, standing up, passed her left—the wet—hand back and forth through the air. With her dry hand, she picked up a congested ashtray from the window seat and carried it with her over to the night table, on which the phone stood. She sat down on one of the made-up twin beds and—it was the fifth or sixth ring—picked up the phone.

"Hello," she said, keeping the fingers of her left hand outstretched and away from her white silk dressing gown, which was all that she was wearing, except mules—her rings were in the bathroom.

"I have your call to New York now, Mrs. Glass," the operator said.

"Thank you," said the girl, and made room on the night table for the ashtray.

A woman's voice came through. "Muriel? Is that you?"

The girl turned the receiver slightly away from her ear. "Yes, Mother. How are you?" she said.

"I've been worried to death about you. Why haven't you phoned? Are you all right?"

"I tried to get you last night and the night before. The phone here's been—"

"Are you all right, Muriel?"

The girl increased the angle between the receiver and her ear. "I'm fine. I'm hot. This is the hottest day they've had in Florida in—"

"Why haven't you called me? I've been worried to—"

"Mother, darling, don't yell at me. I can hear you beautifully," said the girl. "I called you twice last night. Once just after—"

"I *told* your father you'd probably call last night. But, no, he had to—Are you all right, Muriel? Tell me the truth."

"I'm fine. Stop asking me that, please."

"When did you get there?"

"I don't know. Wednesday morning, early."

"Who drove?"

"He did," said the girl. "And don't get excited. He drove very nicely. I was amazed."

"*He* drove? Muriel, you gave me your word of—"

"Mother," the girl interrupted, "I just told you. He drove *very* nicely. Under fifty the whole way, as a matter of fact."

"Did he try any of that funny business with the trees?"

"I *said* he drove very nicely, Mother. Now, please. I asked him to stay close to the white line, and all, and he knew what I meant, and he did. He was even trying not to look at the trees—you could tell. Did Daddy get the car fixed, incidentally?"

"Not yet. They want four hundred dollars, just to—"

"Mother, Seymour *told* Daddy that he'd pay for it. There's no reason for—"

"Well, we'll see. How did he behave—in the car and all?"

"All right," said the girl.

"Did he keep calling you that awful—"

"No. He has something new now."

"What?"

"Oh, what's the *difference*, Mother?"

"Muriel, I want to *know*. Your father—"

"All right, all right. He calls me Miss Spiritual Tramp of 1948," the girl said, and giggled.

"It isn't funny, Muriel. It isn't funny at all. It's horrible. It's *sad,* actually. When I think how—"

"Mother," the girl interrupted, "listen to me. You remember that book he sent me from Germany? You know—those German poems. What'd I *do* with it? I've been racking my—"

"You have it."

"Are you *sure?*" said the girl.

"Certainly. That is, I have it. It's in Freddy's room. You left it here and I didn't have room for it in the— Why? Does he want it?"

"No. Only, he *asked* me about it, when we were driving down. He wanted to know if I'd read it."

"It was in German!"

"Yes, dear. That doesn't make any difference," said the girl, crossing her legs. "He said that the poems happen to be written by the *only great poet of the century*. He said I should've bought a translation or something. Or *learned the language,* if you please."

"Awful. Awful. It's *sad,* actually, is what it is. Your father said last night—"

"Just a second, Mother," the girl said. She went over to the window seat for her cigarettes, lit one, and returned to her seat on the bed. "Mother?" she said, exhaling smoke.

"Muriel. Now, listen to me."

"I'm listening."

"Your father talked to Dr. Sivetski."

"Oh?" said the girl.

"He told him *every*thing. At least, he said he did —you know your father. The trees. That business with the window. Those horrible things he said to Granny about her plans for passing away. What he did with all those lovely pictures from Bermuda—*every*thing."

"Well?" said the girl.

"Well. In the first place, he said it was a perfect *crime* the Army released him from the hospital—my word of honor. He very *definitely* told your father there's a chance—a very *great* chance, he said—that Seymour may com*plete*ly lose control of himself. My word of honor."

"There's a psychiatrist here at the hotel," said the girl.

"*Who?* What's his name?"

"I don't know. Rieser or something. He's supposed to be very good."

"Never heard of him."

"Well, he's supposed to be very good, anyway."

"Muriel, don't be fresh, please. We're *very* worried about you. Your father wanted to wire you *last night* to come home, as a matter of f—"

"I'm not coming home right now, Mother. So relax."

"Muriel. My word of honor. Dr. Sivetski said Seymour may com*plete*ly lose contr—"

"I just *got* here, Mother. This is the first vacation I've had in years, and I'm not going to just *pack* everything and come home," said the girl. "I couldn't travel now anyway. I'm so sunburned I can hardly move."

"You're badly sunburned? Didn't you use that jar of Bronze I put in your bag? I put it right—"

"I used it. I'm burned anyway."

"That's terrible. Where are you burned?"

"All over, dear, all over."

"That's terrible."

"I'll live."

"Tell me, did you talk to this psychiatrist?"

"Well, sort of," said the girl.

"What'd he say? Where was Seymour when you talked to him?"

"In the Ocean Room, playing the piano. He's played the piano both nights we've been here."

"Well, what'd he say?"

"Oh, nothing much. He spoke to me first. I was sitting next to him at Bingo last night, and he asked me if that wasn't my husband playing the piano in the other room. I said yes, it was, and he asked me if Seymour's been sick or something. So I said—"

"Why'd he ask that?"

"*I* don't know, Mother. I guess because he's so pale and all," said the girl. "Anyway, after Bingo he and his wife asked me if I wouldn't like to join them for a drink. So I did. His wife was horrible. You remember that awful dinner dress we saw in Bonwit's window? The one you said you'd have to have a tiny, tiny—"

"The green?"

"She had it on. And all hips. She kept asking me if Seymour's related to that Suzanne Glass that has that place on Madison Avenue—the millinery."

"What'd he say, though? The doctor."

"Oh. Well, nothing much, really. I mean we were in the bar and all. It was terribly noisy."

"Yes, but did—did you tell him what he tried to do with Granny's chair?"

"*No,* Mother. I didn't go into details very much," said the girl. "I'll probably get a chance to talk to him again. He's in the bar *all* day long."

"Did he say he thought there was a chance he might get—you know—funny or anything? Do something to you!"

"Not exactly," said the girl. "He had to have more facts, Mother. They have to know about your childhood—all that stuff. I told you, we could hardly talk, it was so noisy in there."

"Well. How's your blue coat?"

"All right. I had some of the padding taken out."

"How *are* the clothes this year?"

"Terrible. But out of this world. You see sequins—everything," said the girl.

"How's your room?"

"All right. *Just* all right, though. We couldn't get the room we had before the war," said the girl. "The people are awful this year. You should see what sits next to us in the dining room. At the next table. They look as if they drove down in a truck."

"Well, it's that way all over. How's your ballerina?"

"It's too long. I *told* you it was too long."

"Muriel, I'm only going to ask you once more—are you really all right?"

"*Yes,* Mother," said the girl. "For the ninetieth time."

"And you don't want to come home?"

"*No,* Mother."

"Your father said last night that he'd be more than willing to pay for it if you'd go away someplace by yourself and think things over. You could take a lovely cruise. We both thought—"

"No, thanks," said the girl, and uncrossed her legs. "Mother, this call is costing a for—"

"When I think of how you waited for that boy *all* through the war—I mean when you think of all those crazy little wives who—"

"Mother," said the girl, "we'd better hang up. Seymour may come in any minute."

"Where is he?"

"On the beach."

"On the beach? By himself? Does he behave himself on the beach?"

"Mother," said the girl, "you talk about him as though he were a raving *maniac*—"

"I said nothing of the kind, Muriel."

"Well, you *sound* that way. I mean all he does is lie there. He won't take his bathrobe off."

"He won't take his bathrobe off? Why not?"

"*I* don't know. I guess because he's so pale."

"My goodness, he *needs* the sun. Can't you make him?"

"You know Seymour," said the girl, and crossed her legs again. "He says he doesn't want a lot of fools looking at his tattoo."

"He doesn't have any tattoo! Did he get one in the Army?"

"No, Mother. No, dear," said the girl, and stood up. "Listen, I'll call you tomorrow, maybe."

"Muriel. Now, listen to me."

"Yes, Mother," said the girl, putting her weight on her right leg.

"Call me the *instant* he does, or *says,* anything at all funny—you know what I mean. Do you hear me?"

"Mother, I'm not afraid of Seymour."

"Muriel, I want you to promise me."

"All right, I promise. Goodbye, Mother," said the girl. "My love to Daddy." She hung up.

"See more glass," said Sybil Carpenter, who was staying at the hotel with her mother. "Did you see more glass?"

"Pussycat, stop saying that. It's driving Mommy absolutely crazy. Hold still, please."

Mrs. Carpenter was putting sun-tan oil on Sybil's shoulders, spreading it down over the delicate, wing-like blades of her back. Sybil was sitting insecurely on a huge, inflated beach ball, facing the ocean. She was wearing a canary-yellow two-piece bathing suit, one piece of which she would not actually be needing for another nine or ten years.

"It was really just an ordinary silk handkerchief—you could see when you got up close," said the woman in the beach chair beside Mrs. Carpenter's. "I wish I knew how she tied it. It was really darling."

"It sounds darling," Mrs. Carpenter agreed. "Sybil, *hold still*, pussy."

"Did you see more glass?" said Sybil.

Mrs. Carpenter sighed. "All right," she said. She replaced the cap on the sun-tan oil bottle. "Now run and play, pussy. Mommy's going up to the hotel and have a Martini with Mrs. Hubbel. I'll bring you the olive."

Set loose, Sybil immediately ran down to the flat part of the beach and began to walk in the direction of Fisherman's Pavilion. Stopping only to sink a foot in a soggy, collapsed castle, she was soon out of the area reserved for guests of the hotel.

She walked for about a quarter of a mile and then suddenly broke into an oblique run up the soft part of the beach. She stopped short when she reached the place where a young man was lying on his back.

"Are you going in the water, see more glass?" she said.

The young man started, his right hand going to the lapels of his terry-cloth robe. He turned over on his stomach, letting a sausaged towel fall away from his eyes, and squinted up at Sybil.

"Hey. Hello, Sybil."

"Are you going in the water?"

"I was waiting for *you*," said the young man. "What's new?"

"What?" said Sybil.

"What's new? What's on the program?"

"My daddy's coming tomorrow on a nairiplane," Sybil said, kicking sand.

"Not in my face, baby," the young man said, putting his hand on Sybil's ankle. "Well, it's about time he got here, your daddy. I've been expecting him hourly. Hourly."

"Where's the lady?" Sybil said.

"The lady?" the young man brushed some sand out of his thin hair. "That's hard to say, Sybil. She may be in any one of a thousand places. At the hairdresser's. Having her hair dyed mink. Or making dolls for poor children, in her room." Lying prone now, he made two fists, set one on top of the other, and rested his chin on the top one. "Ask me something else, Sybil," he said. "That's a fine bathing suit you have on. If there's one thing I like, it's a blue bathing suit."

Sybil stared at him, then looked down at her protruding stomach. "This is a *yellow,*" she said. "This is a *yellow.*"

"It is? Come a little closer."

Sybil took a step forward.

"You're absolutely right. What a fool I am."

"Are you going in the water?" Sybil said.

"I'm seriously considering it. I'm giving it plenty of thought, Sybil, you'll be glad to know."

Sybil prodded the rubber float that the young man sometimes used as a head-rest. "It needs *air,*" she said.

"You're right. It needs more air than I'm willing to admit." He took away his fists and let his chin rest on the sand. "Sybil," he said, "you're looking fine. It's good to see you. Tell me about yourself." He reached in front of him and took both of Sybil's ankles in his hands. "I'm Capricorn," he said. "What are you?"

"Sharon Lipschutz said you let her sit on the piano seat with you," Sybil said.

"Sharon Lipschutz said that?"

Sybil nodded vigorously.

He let go of her ankles, drew in his hands, and

laid the side of his face on his right forearm. "Well," he said, "you know how those things happen, Sybil. I was sitting there, playing. And you were nowhere in sight. And Sharon Lipschutz came over and sat down next to me. I couldn't push her off, could I?"

"Yes."

"Oh, no. No. I couldn't do that," said the young man. "I'll tell you what I did do, though."

"What?"

"I pretended she was you."

Sybil immediately stooped and began to dig in the sand. "Let's go in the water," she said.

"All right," said the young man. "I think I can work it in."

"Next time, push her off," Sybil said.

"Push who off?"

"Sharon Lipschutz."

"Ah, Sharon Lipschutz," said the young man. "How that name comes up. Mixing memory and desire." He suddenly got to his feet. He looked at the ocean. "Sybil," he said, "I'll tell you what we'll do. We'll see if we can catch a bananafish."

"A what?"

"A bananafish," he said, and undid the belt of his robe. He took off the robe. His shoulders were white and narrow, and his trunks were royal blue. He folded the robe, first lengthwise, then in thirds. He unrolled the towel he had used over his eyes, spread it out on the sand, and then laid the folded robe on top of it. He bent over, picked up the float, and secured it under his right arm. Then, with his left hand, he took Sybil's hand.

The two started to walk down to the ocean.

"I imagine you've seen quite a few bananafish in your day," the young man said.

Sybil shook her head.

"You haven't? Where do you *live,* anyway?"

"I don't know," said Sybil.

"Sure you know. You must know. Sharon Lipschutz knows where *she* lives and *she's* only *three and a half.*"

Sybil stopped walking and yanked her hand away from him. She picked up an ordinary beach shell and looked at it with elaborate interest. She threw it down. "Whirly Wood, Connecticut," she said, and resumed walking, stomach foremost.

"Whirly Wood, Connecticut," said the young man. "Is that anywhere near Whirly Wood, Connecticut, by any chance?"

Sybil looked at him. "That's where I *live,*" she said impatiently. "I *live* in Whirly Wood, Connecticut." She ran a few steps ahead of him, caught up her left foot in her left hand, and hopped two or three times.

"You have no idea how clear that makes everything," the young man said.

Sybil released her foot. "Did you read 'Little Black Sambo'?" she said.

"It's very funny you ask me that," he said. "It so happens I just finished reading it last night." He reached down and took back Sybil's hand. "What did you think of it?" he asked her.

"Did the tigers run all around that tree?"

"I thought they'd never stop. I never saw so many tigers."

"There were only six," Sybil said.

"*Only* six!" said the young man. "Do you call that *only?*"

"Do you like wax?" Sybil asked.

"Do I like what?" asked the young man.

"Wax."

"Very much. Don't you?"

Sybil nodded. "Do you like olives?" she asked.

"Olives—yes. Olives and wax. I never go anyplace without 'em."

"Do you like Sharon Lipschutz?" Sybil asked.

"Yes. Yes, I do," said the young man. "What I like par*ti*cularly about her is that she never does anything mean to little dogs in the lobby of the hotel. That little toy bull that belongs to that lady from Canada, for instance. You probably won't believe this, but *some* little girls like to poke that little dog with balloon sticks. Sharon doesn't. She's never mean or unkind. That's why I like her so much."

Sybil was silent.

"I like to chew candles," she said finally.

"Who doesn't?" said the young man, getting his feet wet. "Wow! It's cold." He dropped the rubber float on its back. "No, wait just a second, Sybil. Wait'll we get out a little bit."

They waded out till the water was up to Sybil's waist. Then the young man picked her up and laid her down on her stomach on the float.

"Don't you ever wear a bathing cap or anything?" he asked.

"Don't let go," Sybil ordered. "You hold me, now."

"Miss Carpenter. Please. I know my business," the young man said. "You just keep your eyes open for any bananafish. This is a *perfect* day for bananafish."

"I don't see any," Sybil said.

"That's understandable. Their habits are *very* peculiar." He kept pushing the float. The water was not quite up to his chest. "They lead a very tragic life," he said. "You know what they do, Sybil?"

She shook her head.

"Well, they swim into a hole where there's a lot

of bananas. They're very ordinary-looking fish when they swim *in*. But once they get in, they behave like pigs. Why, I've known some bananafish to swim into a banana hole and eat as many as seventy-eight bananas." He edged the float and its passenger a foot closer to the horizon. "Naturally, after that they're so fat they can't get out of the hole again. Can't fit through the door."

"Not too far out," Sybil said. "What happens to them?"

"What happens to who?"

"The bananafish."

"Oh, you mean after they eat so many bananas they can't get out of the banana hole?"

"Yes," said Sybil.

"Well, I hate to tell you, Sybil. They die."

"Why?" asked Sybil.

"Well, they get banana fever. It's a terrible disease."

"Here comes a *wave*," Sybil said nervously.

"We'll ignore it. We'll snub it," said the young man. "Two snobs." He took Sybil's ankles in his hands and pressed down and forward. The float nosed over the top of the wave. The water soaked Sybil's blond hair, but her scream was full of pleasure.

With her hand, when the float was level again, she wiped away a flat, wet band of hair from her eyes, and reported, "I just saw one."

"Saw what, my love?"

"A bananafish."

"My God, no!" said the young man. "Did he have any bananas in his mouth?"

"Yes," said Sybil. "Six."

The young man suddenly picked up one of Sybil's

wet feet, which were drooping over the end of the float, and kissed the arch.

"Hey!" said the owner of the foot, turning around.

"Hey, yourself! We're going in now. You had enough?"

"No!"

"Sorry," he said, and pushed the float toward shore until Sybil got off it. He carried it the rest of the way.

"Goodbye," said Sybil, and ran without regret in the direction of the hotel.

The young man put on his robe, closed the lapels tight, and jammed his towel into his pocket. He picked up the slimy wet, cumbersome float and put it under his arm. He plodded alone through the soft, hot sand toward the hotel.

On the sub-main floor of the hotel, which the management directed bathers to use, a woman with zinc salve on her nose got into the elevator with the young man.

"I see you're looking at my feet," he said to her when the car was in motion.

"I beg your pardon?" said the woman.

"I said I see you're looking at my feet."

"I *beg* your pardon. I happened to be looking at the floor," said the woman, and faced the doors of the car.

"If you want to look at my feet, say so," said the young man. "But don't be a God-damned sneak about it."

"Let me out here, please," the woman said quickly to the girl operating the car.

The car doors opened and the woman got out without looking back.

"I have two normal feet and I can't see the slightest God-damned reason why anybody should stare at them," said the young man. "Five, please." He took his room key out of his robe pocket.

He got off at the fifth floor, walked down the hall, and let himself into 507. The room smelled of new calfskin luggage and nail-lacquer remover.

He glanced at the girl lying asleep on one of the twin beds. Then he went over to one of the pieces of luggage, opened it, and from under a pile of shorts and undershirts he took out an Ortgies calibre 7.65 automatic. He released the magazine, looked at it, then reinserted it. He cocked the piece. Then he went over and sat down on the unoccupied twin bed, looked at the girl, aimed the pistol, and fired a bullet through his right temple.

Uncle Wiggily in Connecticut

IT WAS ALMOST THREE O'CLOCK when Mary Jane finally found Eloise's house. She explained to Eloise, who had come out to the driveway to meet her, that everything had been absolutely *perfect*, that she had remembered the way *exactly*, until she had turned off the Merrick Parkway. Eloise said, "*Merritt* Parkway, baby," and reminded Mary Jane that she had found the house twice before, but Mary Jane just wailed something ambiguous, something about her box of Kleenex, and rushed back to her convertible. Eloise turned up the collar of her camel's-hair coat, put her back to the wind, and waited. Mary Jane was back in a minute using a leaf of Kleenex and still looking upset, even fouled. Eloise said cheerfully that the whole damn lunch was burned—sweetbreads, everything—but Mary Jane said she'd eaten anyway, on the road. As the two walked toward the house, Eloise asked Mary Jane how it happened she had the day off. Mary Jane said she didn't have the *whole* day off; it was just that Mr. Weyinburg had a hernia and was home in Larchmont, and she had to bring him his mail and take a couple of letters every afternoon. She asked Eloise, "Just exactly what *is* a hernia, anyway?" Eloise, dropping her cigarette on the soiled snow underfoot, said she didn't *actually* know but that Mary Jane didn't have to worry much about getting one. Mary Jane said, "Oh," and the two girls entered the house.

Twenty minutes later, they were finishing their first highball in the living room and were talking in the manner peculiar, probably limited, to former college roommates. They had an even stronger bond between them; neither of them had graduated. Eloise had left college in the middle of her sophomore year, in 1942, a week after she had been caught with a soldier in a closed elevator on the third floor of her residence hall. Mary Jane had left—same year, same class, almost the same month—to marry an aviation cadet stationed in Jacksonville, Florida, a lean, air-minded boy from Dill, Mississippi, who had spent two of the three months Mary Jane had been married to him in jail for stabbing an M.P.

"No," Eloise was saying. "It was actually *red*." She was stretched out on the couch, her thin but very pretty legs crossed at the ankles.

"I heard it was blond," Mary Jane repeated. She was seated in the blue straight chair. "Wuddayacallit swore up and down it was blond."

"Uh-uh. Definitely." Eloise yawned. "I was almost in the *room* with her when she dyed it. What's the matter? Aren't there any cigarettes in there?"

"It's all right. I have a whole pack," Mary Jane said. "Somewhere." She searched through her handbag.

"That dopey maid," Eloise said without moving from the couch. "I dropped two brand-new cartons in front of her nose about an hour ago. She'll be in, any minute, to ask me what to do with them. Where the hell was I?"

"Thieringer," Mary Jane prompted, lighting one of her own cigarettes.

"Oh, yeah. I remember exactly. She dyed it the *night* before she married that Frank Henke. You remember him at all?"

"Just sort of. Little ole private? Terribly unattractive?"

"Unattractive. God! He looked like an unwashed Bela Lugosi."

Mary Jane threw back her head and roared. "Marvellous," she said, coming back into drinking position.

"Gimme your glass," Eloise said, swinging her stockinged feet to the floor and standing up. "Honestly, that *dope*. I did everything but get Lew to make love to her to get her to come out here with us. Now I'm sorry I—Where'd you get that thing?"

"*This?*" said Mary Jane, touching a cameo brooch at her throat. "I had it at school, for goodness sake. It was Mother's."

"God," Eloise said, with the empty glasses in her hands. "I don't have one damn thing holy to wear. If Lew's mother ever dies—ha, ha—she'll probably leave me some old monogrammed icepick or something."

"How're you getting along with her these days, anyway?"

"Don't be funny," Eloise said on her way to the kitchen.

"This is positively the last one for me!" Mary Jane called after her.

"Like hell it is. *Who* called *who*? And who came two hours late? You're gonna stick around till I'm sick of you. The hell with your lousy career."

Mary Jane threw back her head and roared again, but Eloise had already gone into the kitchen.

With little or no wherewithal for being left alone in a room, Mary Jane stood up and walked over to the window. She drew aside the curtain and leaned her wrist on one of the crosspieces between panes, but, feeling grit, she removed it, rubbed it clean with her other hand, and stood up more erectly. Outside, the filthy slush was visibly turning to ice. Mary Jane let go the curtain and wandered back to the blue chair, passing two heavily stocked bookcases without glancing at any of the titles. Seated, she opened her handbag and used the mirror to look at her teeth. She closed her lips and ran her tongue hard over her upper front teeth, then took another look.

"It's getting so *icy* out," she said, turning. "God, that was quick. Didn't you put any soda in them?"

Eloise, with a fresh drink in each hand, stopped short. She extended both index fingers, gun-muzzle style, and said, "Don't nobody move. I got the whole damn place surrounded."

Mary Jane laughed and put away her mirror.

Eloise came forward with the drinks. She placed Mary Jane's insecurely in its coaster but kept her own in hand. She stretched out on the couch again. "Wuddaya think she's doing out there?" she said. "She's sitting on her big, black butt reading 'The Robe.' I dropped the ice trays taking them out. She actually looked up annoyed."

"This is my last. And I mean it," Mary Jane said, picking up her drink. "Oh, listen! You know who I saw last week? On the main floor of Lord & Taylor's?"

"Mm-hm," said Eloise, adjusting a pillow under her head. "Akim Tamiroff."

"Who?" said Mary Jane. "Who's he?"

"Akim Tamiroff. He's in the movies. He always says, 'You make beeg joke—hah?' I love him. . . . There isn't one damn pillow in this house that I can stand. Who'd you see?"

"Jackson. She was—"

"Which one?"

"I don't know. The one that was in our Psych class, that always—"

"Both of them were in our Psych class."

"Well. The one with the terrific—"

"Marcia Louise. I ran into her once, too. She talk your ear off?"

"God, yes. But you know what she told me, though? Dr. Whiting's dead. She said she had a letter from Barbara Hill saying Whiting got cancer last summer and died and all. She only weighed sixty-two pounds. When she died. Isn't that terrible?"

"No."

"Eloise, you're getting hard as nails."

"Mm. What else'd she say?"

"Oh, she just got back from Europe. Her husband was stationed in Germany or something, and she was with him. They had a forty-seven-room house, she said, just with one other couple, and about ten servants. Her own horse, and the groom they had, used to be Hitler's own private riding master or something. Oh, and she started to tell me how she almost got raped by a colored soldier. *Right* on the main floor of Lord & Taylor's she started to tell me—you know Jackson. She said he was her husband's chauffeur, and he was driving her to market or something one morning. She said she was so scared she didn't even—"

"Wait just a second." Eloise raised her head and her voice. "Is that you, Ramona?"

"Yes," a small child's voice answered.

"Close the front door after you, please," Eloise called.

"Is that Ramona? Oh, I'm dying to see her. Do you realize I haven't seen her since she had her—"

"Ramona," Eloise shouted, with her eyes shut, "go out in the kitchen and let Grace take your galoshes off."

"All right," said Ramona. "C'mon, Jimmy."

"Oh, I'm dying to see her," Mary Jane said. "Oh, *God!* Look what I did. I'm *ter*ribly sorry, El."

"Leave it. *Leave* it," said Eloise. "I hate this damn rug anyway. I'll get you another."

"No, look, I have more than half left!" Mary Jane held up her glass.

"Sure?" said Eloise. "Gimme a cigarette."

Mary Jane extended her pack of cigarettes, saying "Oh, I'm dying to see her. Who does she look like now?"

Eloise struck a light. "Akim Tamiroff."

"No, seriously."

"Lew. She looks like Lew. When his mother comes over, the three of them look like triplets." Without sitting up, Eloise reached for a stack of ashtrays on the far side of the cigarette table. She successfully lifted off the top one and set it down on her stomach. "What I need is a cocker spaniel or something," she said. "Somebody that looks like me."

"How're her eyes now?" Mary Jane asked. "I mean they're not any worse or anything, are they?"

"God! Not that I know of."

"Can she see at all without her glasses? I mean if she gets up in the night to go to the john or something?"

"She won't tell anybody. She's lousy with secrets."

Mary Jane turned around in her chair. "Well, he*llo*, Ramona!" she said. "Oh, what a *pretty* dress!" She set down her drink. "I'll bet you don't even remember me, Ramona."

"Certainly she does. Who's the lady, Ramona?"

"Mary Jane," said Ramona, and scratched herself.

"Marvellous!" said Mary Jane. "Ramona, will you give me a little kiss?"

"Stop that," Eloise said to Ramona.

Ramona stopped scratching herself.

"Will you give me a little kiss, Ramona?" Mary Jane asked again.

"I don't like to kiss people."

Eloise snorted, and asked, "Where's Jimmy?"

"He's here."

"Who's Jimmy?" Mary Jane asked Eloise.

"Oh, God! Her beau. Goes where she goes. Does what she does. All very hoopla."

"*Really?*" said Mary Jane enthusiastically. She leaned forward. "Do you have a beau, Ramona?"

Ramona's eyes, behind thick, counter-myopia lenses, did not reflect even the smallest part of Mary Jane's enthusiasm.

"Mary Jane asked you a question, Ramona," Eloise said.

Ramona inserted a finger into her small, broad nose.

"Stop that," Eloise said. "Mary Jane asked you if you have a beau."

"Yes," said Ramona, busy with her nose.

"Ramona," Eloise said. "Cut that out. But immediately."

Ramona put her hand down.

"Well, I think that's just wonderful," Mary Jane said. "What's his name? Will you tell me his name, Ramona? Or is it a big secret?"

"Jimmy," Ramona said.

"Jimmy? Oh, I love the name Jimmy! Jimmy what, Ramona?"

"Jimmy Jimmereeno," said Ramona.

"Stand still," said Eloise.

"Well! That's quite a name. Where is Jimmy? Will you tell me, Ramona?"

"Here," said Ramona.

Mary Jane looked around, then looked back at Ramona, smiling as provocatively as possible. "Here where, honey?"

"Here," said Ramona. "I'm holding his *hand.*"

"I don't get it," Mary Jane said to Eloise, who was finishing her drink.

"Don't look at *me,*" said Eloise.

Mary Jane looked back at Ramona. "Oh, *I* see. Jimmy's just a make-believe little boy. Marvellous." Mary Jane leaned forward cordially. "How do you *do,* Jimmy?" she said.

"He won't talk to you," said Eloise. "Ramona, tell Mary Jane about Jimmy."

"Tell her *what?*"

"Stand up, please. . . . Tell Mary Jane how Jimmy looks."

"He has green eyes and black hair."

"What else?"

"No mommy and no daddy."

"What else?"

"No freckles."

"What else?"

"A sword."

"What else?"

"I don't know," said Ramona, and began to scratch herself again.

"He sounds *beau*tiful!" Mary Jane said, and leaned even farther forward in her chair. "Ramona. Tell me. Did Jimmy take off *his* galoshes, too, when you came in?"

"He has boots," Ramona said.

"Marvellous," Mary Jane said to Eloise.

"You just think so. I get it all day long. Jimmy eats with her. Takes a bath with her. Sleeps with her. She sleeps way over to one side of the bed, so's not to roll over and hurt him."

Looking absorbed and delighted with this information, Mary Jane took in her lower lip, then released it to ask, "Where'd he get that name, though?"

"Jimmy Jimmereeno? God knows."

"Probably from some little boy in the neighborhood."

Eloise, yawning, shook her head. "There are no little boys in the neighborhood. No children at all. They call me Fertile Fanny behind my—"

"Mommy," Ramona said, "can I go out and play?"

Eloise looked at her. "You just came *in*," she said.

"Jimmy wants to go out again."

"Why, may I ask?"

"He left his sword outside."

"Oh, him and his goddam sword," Eloise said. "Well. Go ahead. Put your galoshes back on."

"Can I have this?" Ramona said, taking a burned match out of the ashtray.

"*May* I have this. Yes. Stay out of the street, please."

"Goodbye, Ramona!" Mary Jane said musically.

"Bye," said Ramona. "C'mon, Jimmy."

Eloise lunged suddenly to her feet. "Gimme your glass," she said.

"No, really, El. I'm supposed to be in *Larchmont*. I mean Mr. Weyinburg's *so* sweet, I hate to—"

"Call up and say you were killed. Let go of that damn glass."

"No, honestly, El. I mean it's getting so *terribly* icy. I have hardly any anti-freeze in the car. I mean if I don't—"

"Let it freeze. Go phone. Say you're dead," said Eloise. "Gimme that."

"Well . . . Where's the phone?"

"It went," said Eloise, carrying the empty glasses and walking toward the dining room, "—this-a-way." She stopped short on the floor board between the living room and the dining room and executed a grind and a bump. Mary Jane giggled.

"I mean you didn't really *know* Walt," said Eloise at a quarter of five, lying on her back on the floor, a drink balanced upright on her small-breasted chest. "He was the only boy I ever knew that could make me laugh. I mean *really* laugh." She looked over at Mary Jane. "You remember that night—our last year— when that crazy Louise Hermanson busted in the room wearing that black brassière she bought in Chicago?"

Mary Jane giggled. She was lying on her stomach on the couch, her chin on the armrest, facing Eloise. Her drink was on the floor, within reach.

"Well, he could make me laugh *that* way," Eloise said. "He could do it when he talked to me. He could do it over the phone. He could even do it in a letter. And the best thing about it was that he didn't even try to be funny—he just *was* funny." She turned her head slightly toward Mary Jane. "Hey, how 'bout throwing me a cigarette?"

"I can't reach 'em," Mary Jane said.

"Nuts to you." Eloise looked up at the ceiling again. "Once," she said, "I fell down. I used to wait for him at the bus stop, right outside the PX, and he showed up late once, just as the bus was pulling out. We started to run for it, and I fell and twisted my ankle. He said, 'Poor Uncle Wiggily.' He meant my ankle. Poor old Uncle Wiggily, he called it. . . . God, he was nice."

"Doesn't Lew have a sense of humor?" Mary Jane said.

"What?"

"Doesn't Lew have a sense of humor?"

"Oh, God! Who knows? Yes. I guess so. He laughs at cartoons and stuff." Eloise raised her head, lifted her drink from her chest, and drank from it.

"Well," Mary Jane said. "That isn't everything. I mean that isn't everything."

"What isn't?"

"Oh . . . you know. Laughing and stuff."

"Who says it isn't?" Eloise said. "Listen, if you're not gonna be a nun or something, you might as well laugh."

Mary Jane giggled. "You're *terr*ible," she said.

"Ah, God, he was nice," Eloise said. "He was either funny or sweet. Not that damn little-boy sweet, either. It was a special kind of sweet. You know what he did once?"

"Uh-uh," Mary Jane said.

"We were on the train going from Trenton to New York—it was just right after he was drafted. It was cold in the car and I had my coat sort of over us. I remember I had Joyce Morrow's cardigan on underneath—you remember that darling blue cardigan she had?"

Mary Jane nodded, but Eloise didn't look over to get the nod.

"Well, he sort of had his hand on my stomach. You know. Anyway, all of a sudden he said my stomach was so beautiful he wished some officer would come up and order him to stick his other hand through the window. He said he wanted to do what was fair. Then he took his hand away and told the conductor to throw his shoulders back. He told him if there was one thing he couldn't stand it was a man who didn't look proud of his uniform. The conductor just told him to go back to sleep." Eloise reflected a moment, then said, "It wasn't always what he said, but how he said it. You know."

"Have you ever told Lew about him—I mean, at all?"

"Oh," Eloise said, "I started to, once. But the first thing he asked me was what his rank was."

"What was his rank?"

"Ha!" said Eloise.

"No, I just meant—"

Eloise laughed suddenly, from her diaphragm. "You know what he said once? He said he felt he was advancing in the Army, but in a different direction from everybody else. He said that when he'd get his first promotion, instead of getting stripes he'd have his sleeves taken away from him. He said when he'd get to be a general, he'd be stark naked. All he'd be wearing would be a little infantry button in his navel." Eloise looked over at Mary Jane, who wasn't laughing. "Don't you think that's funny?"

"Yes. Only, why don't you tell Lew about him some-time, though?"

"Why? Because he's too damn unintelligent, that's why," Eloise said. "Besides. Listen to me, career girl. If you ever get married again, don't tell your husband *anything*. Do you hear me?"

"Why?" said Mary Jane.

"Because I say so, that's why," said Eloise. "They wanna think you spent your whole life vomiting every time a boy came near you. I'm not kidding, either. Oh, you can tell them stuff. But never honestly. I mean never *honestly*. If you tell 'em you once knew a handsome boy, you gotta say in the same breath he was *too* handsome. And if you tell 'em you knew a witty boy, you gotta tell 'em he was kind of a smart aleck, though, or a wise guy. If you *don't*, they hit you over the head with the poor boy every time they get a chance." Eloise paused to drink from her glass and to think. "Oh," she said, "they'll listen very *maturely* and all that. They'll even look intelligent as hell. But don't let it fool you. Believe me. You'll go through *hell* if you ever give 'em any credit for intelligence. Take my word."

Mary Jane, looking depressed, raised her chin from the armrest of the couch. For a change, she supported her chin on her forearm. She thought over Eloise's advice. "You can't call Lew not intelligent," she said aloud.

"Who can't?"

"I mean isn't he intelligent?" Mary Jane said innocently.

"Oh," said Eloise, "what's the use of talking? Let's drop it. I'll just depress you. Shut me up."

"Well, wudga marry him for, then?" Mary Jane said.

"Oh, God! I don't know. He told me he loved Jane Austen. He told me her books meant a great deal to him. That's exactly what he said. I found out after we were married that he hadn't even read *one* of her books. You know who his favorite author is?"

Mary Jane shook her head.

"L. Manning Vines. Ever hear of him?"

"Uh-uh."

"Neither did I. Neither did anybody else. He wrote a book about four men that starved to death in Alaska. Lew doesn't remember the name of it, but it's the most beautifully *written* book he's ever read. *Christ!* He isn't even honest enough to come right out and say he liked it because it was about four guys that starved to death in an igloo or something. He has to say it was beautifully *written*."

"You're too critical," Mary Jane said. "I mean you're too critical. Maybe it *was* a good—"

"Take my word for it, it couldn't've been," Eloise said. She thought for a moment, then added, "At least, you have a job. I mean at least you—"

"But listen, though," said Mary Jane. "Do you think you'll ever tell him Walt was killed, even? I mean he wouldn't be jealous, would he, if he knew Walt was —you know. Killed and everything."

"Oh, lover! You poor, innocent little career girl," said Eloise. "He'd be worse. He'd be a *ghoul*. Listen. All he knows is that I went around with somebody named Walt—some *wisecracking* G.I. The last thing I'd do would be to tell him he was killed. But the last thing. And if I did—which I wouldn't—but if I *did*, I'd tell him he was killed in action."

Mary Jane pushed her chin farther forward over the edge of her forearm.

"El . . ." she said.

"Uh?"

"Why won't you tell me how he was killed? I *swear* I won't tell anybody. Honestly. Please."

"No."

"Please. Honestly. I won't tell anybody."

Eloise finished her drink and replaced the empty glass upright on her chest. "You'd tell Akim Tamiroff," she said.

"No, I wouldn't! I mean I wouldn't tell any—"

"Oh," said Eloise, "his regiment was resting someplace. It was between battles or something, this friend of his said that wrote me. Walt and some other boy were putting this little Japanese stove in a package. Some colonel wanted to send it home. Or they were taking it *out* of the package to rewrap it—I don't know exactly. Anyway, it was all full of gasoline and junk and it exploded in their faces. The other boy just lost an eye." Eloise began to cry. She put her hand around the empty glass on her chest to steady it.

Mary Jane slid off the couch and, on her knees, took three steps over to Eloise and began to stroke her forehead. "Don't cry, El. Don't cry."

"Who's crying?" Eloise said.

"I know, but don't. I mean it isn't worth it or anything."

The front door opened.

"That's Ramona back," Eloise said nasally. "Do me a favor. Go out in the kitchen and tell whosis to give her her dinner early. Willya?"

"All right, if you promise not to cry, though."

"I promise. Go on. I don't feel like going out to that damn kitchen right this minute."

Mary Jane stood up, losing and recovering her balance, and left the room.

She was back in less than two minutes, with Ramona running ahead of her. Ramona ran as flat-footed as possible, trying to get the maximum noise out of her open galoshes.

"She wouldn't let me take her galoshes off," Mary Jane said.

Eloise, still lying on her back on the floor, was using her handkerchief. She spoke into it, addressing Ramona. "Go out and tell Grace to take your galoshes off. You know you're not supposed to come into the—"

"She's in the lavatory," Ramona said.

Eloise put away her handkerchief and hoisted herself to a sitting position. "Gimme your foot," she said. "Sit down, first, please. . . . Not *there—here*. God!"

On her knees, looking under the table for her cigarettes, Mary Jane said, "Hey. Guess what happened to Jimmy."

"No idea. Other foot. *Other* foot."

"He got runned over," said Mary Jane. "Isn't that tragic?"

"I saw Skipper with a bone," Ramona told Eloise.

"What happened to Jimmy?" Eloise said to her.

"He got runned over and killed. I saw Skipper with a bone, and he wouldn't—"

"Gimme your forehead a second," Eloise said. She reached out and felt Ramona's forehead. "You feel a little feverish. Go tell Grace you're to have your dinner upstairs. Then you're to go straight to bed. I'll be up later. Go on, now, please. Take these *with* you."

Ramona slowly giant-stepped her way out of the room.

"Throw me one," Eloise said to Mary Jane. "Let's have another drink."

Mary Jane carried a cigarette over to Eloise. "Isn't that something? About Jimmy? What an imagination!"

"Mm. You go get the drinks, huh? And bring the bottle . . . I don't wanna go out there. The whole damn place smells like orange juice."

At five minutes past seven, the phone rang. Eloise got up from the window seat and felt in the dark for her shoes. She couldn't find them. In her stocking feet, she walked steadily, almost languidly, toward the phone. The ringing didn't disturb Mary Jane, who was asleep on the couch, face down.

"Hello," Eloise said into the phone, without having turned the overhead light on. "Look, I can't meet you. Mary Jane's here. She's got her car parked right in front of me and she can't find the key. I can't get out. We spent about twenty minutes looking for it in the wuddayacallit—the snow and stuff. Maybe you can get a lift with Dick and Mildred." She listened. "Oh. Well, that's tough, kid. Why don't you boys form a platoon and march home? You can say that hut-hope-hoop-hoop business. You can be the big shot." She listened again. "I'm not funny," she said. "Really, I'm not. It's just my face." She hung up.

She walked, less steadily, back into the living room. At the window seat, she poured what was left in the bottle of Scotch into her glass. It made about a finger. She drank it off, shivered, and sat down.

When Grace turned on the light in the dining room, Eloise jumped. Without getting up, she called in to Grace, "You better not serve until eight, Grace. Mr. Wengler'll be a little late."

Grace appeared in the dining-room light but didn't come forward. "The lady go?" she said.

"She's resting."

"Oh," said Grace. "Miz Wengler, I wondered if it'd be all right if my husband passed the evenin' here. I

got plentya room in my room, and he don't have to
be back in New York till tomorrow mornin', and it's
so *bad* out."

"Your husband? Where is he?"

"Well, right now," Grace said, "he's in the kitchen."

"Well, I'm afraid he can't spend the night here,
Grace."

"Ma'am?"

"I say I'm afraid he can't spend the night here. I'm
not running a hotel."

Grace stood for a moment, then said, "Yes, Ma'am,"
and went out to the kitchen.

Eloise left the living room and climbed the stairs,
which were lighted very faintly by the overglow from
the dining room. One of Ramona's galoshes was lying
on the landing. Eloise picked it up and threw it, with
as much force as possible, over the side of the banister; it struck the foyer floor with a violent thump.

She snapped on the light in Ramona's room and
held on to the switch, as if for support. She stood still
for a moment looking at Ramona. Then she let go
of the light switch and went quickly over to the bed.

"Ramona. Wake up. Wake *up*."

Ramona was sleeping far over on one side of the
bed, her right buttock off the edge. Her glasses were
on a little Donald Duck night table, folded neatly and
laid stems down.

"Ramona!"

The child awoke with a sharp intake of breath. Her
eyes opened wide, but she narrowed them almost at
once. "Mommy?"

"I thought you told me Jimmy Jimmereeno was run
over and killed."

"What?"

"You heard me," Eloise said. "Why are you sleeping way over here?"

"Because," said Ramona.

"Because why? Ramona, I don't feel like—"

"Because I don't want to hurt Mickey."

"Who?"

"Mickey," said Ramona, rubbing her nose. "Mickey Mickeranno."

Eloise raised her voice to a shriek. "You get in the center of that bed. *Go on.*"

Ramona, extremely frightened, just looked up at Eloise.

"All right." Eloise grabbed Ramona's ankles and half lifted and half pulled her over to the middle of the bed. Ramona neither struggled nor cried; she let herself be moved without actually submitting to it.

"Now go to sleep," Eloise said, breathing heavily. "Close your eyes. . . . You heard me, *close* them."

Ramona closed her eyes.

Eloise went over to the light switch and flicked it off. But she stood for a long time in the doorway. Then, suddenly, she rushed, in the dark, over to the night table, banging her knee against the foot of the bed, but too full of purpose to feel pain. She picked up Ramona's glasses and, holding them in both hands, pressed them against her cheek. Tears rolled down her face, wetting the lenses. "Poor Uncle Wiggily," she said over and over again. Finally, she put the glasses back on the night table, lenses down.

She stooped over, losing her balance, and began to tuck in the blankets of Ramona's bed. Ramona was awake. She was crying and had been crying. Eloise kissed her wetly on the mouth and wiped the hair out of her eyes and then left the room.

She went downstairs, staggering now very badly, and wakened Mary Jane.

"*Wuzzat?* Who? *Huh?*" said Mary Jane, sitting bolt upright on the couch.

"Mary Jane. Listen. Please," Eloise said, sobbing. "You remember our freshman year, and I had that brown-and-yellow dress I bought in Boise, and Miriam Ball told me nobody wore those kind of dresses in New York, and I cried all night?" Eloise shook Mary Jane's arm. "I was a nice girl," she pleaded, "wasn't I?"

Just Before the War
with the Eskimos

FIVE STRAIGHT SATURDAY MORNINGS, Ginnie Mannox had played tennis at the East Side Courts with Selena Graff, a classmate at Miss Basehoar's. Ginnie openly considered Selena the biggest drip at Miss Basehoar's —a school ostensibly abounding with fair-sized drips —but at the same time she had never known anyone like Selena for bringing fresh cans of tennis balls. Selena's father made them or something. (At dinner one night, for the edification of the entire Mannox family, Ginnie had conjured up a vision of dinner over at the Graffs'; it involved a perfect servant coming around to everyone's left with, instead of a glass of tomato juice, a can of tennis balls.) But this business of dropping Selena off at her house after tennis and then getting stuck—every single time—for the whole cab fare was getting on Ginnie's nerves. After all, taking the taxi home from the courts instead of the bus had been Selena's idea. On the fifth Saturday, however, as the cab started north in York Avenue, Ginnie suddenly spoke up.

"Hey, Selena . . ."

"What?" asked Selena, who was busy feeling the floor of the cab with her hand. "I can't find the cover to my racket!" she moaned.

Despite the warm May weather, both girls were wearing topcoats over their shorts.

"You put it in your pocket," Ginnie said. "Hey, listen—"

"Oh, God! You've saved my life!"

"Listen," said Ginnie, who wanted no part of Selena's gratitude.

"What?"

Ginnie decided to come right out with it. The cab was nearly at Selena's street. "I don't feel like getting stuck for the whole cab fare again today," she said. "I'm no millionaire, ya know."

Selena looked first amazed, then hurt. "Don't I always pay half?" she asked innocently.

"No," said Ginnie flatly. "You paid half the *first* Saturday. Way in the beginning of last month. And since then not even once. I don't wanna be ratty, but I'm actually ex*ist*ing on four-fifty a week. And out of that I have to—"

"I always bring the tennis balls, don't I?" Selena asked unpleasantly.

Sometimes Ginnie felt like killing Selena. "Your father *makes* them or something," she said. "They don't cost *you* anything. I have to pay for every single little—"

"All right, all right," Selena said, loudly and with finality enough to give herself the upper hand. Looking bored, she went through the pockets of her coat. "I only have thirty-five cents," she said coldly. "Is that enough?"

"No. I'm sorry, but you owe me a dollar sixty-five. I've been keeping track of every—"

"I'll have to go upstairs and get it from my mother. Can't it wait till *Monday?* I could bring it to *gym* with me if it'd make you happy."

Selena's attitude defied clemency.

"No," Ginnie said. "I have to go to the movies to-night. I need it."

In hostile silence, the girls stared out of opposite windows until the cab pulled up in front of Selena's apartment house. Then Selena, who was seated near-est the curb, let herself out. Just barely leaving the cab door open, she walked briskly and obliviously, like visiting Hollywood royalty, into the building. Ginnie, her face burning, paid the fare. She then collected her tennis things—racket, hand towel, and sun hat—and followed Selena. At fifteen, Ginnie was about five feet nine in her 9-B tennis shoes, and as she entered the lobby, her self-conscious rubber-soled awkwardness lent her a dangerous amateur quality. It made Selena prefer to watch the indicator dial over the elevator.

"That makes a dollar ninety you owe me," Ginnie said, striding up to the elevator.

Selena turned. "It may just interest you to know," she said, "that my mother is very ill."

"What's the matter with her?"

"She virtually has pneumonia, and if you think I'm going to enjoy disturbing her just for money . . ." Selena delivered the incomplete sentence with all possible aplomb.

Ginnie was, in fact, slightly put off by this informa-tion, whatever its degree of truth, but not to the point of sentimentality. "I didn't give it to her," she said, and followed Selena into the elevator.

When Selena had rung her apartment bell, the girls

were admitted—or rather, the door was drawn in and left ajar—by a colored maid with whom Selena didn't seem to be on speaking terms. Ginnie dropped her tennis things on a chair in the foyer and followed Selena. In the living room, Selena turned and said, "Do you mind waiting here? I *may* have to wake Mother up and everything."

"O.K.," Ginnie said, and plopped down on the sofa.

"I never in my life would've thought you could be so small about anything," said Selena, who was just angry enough to use the word "small" but not quite brave enough to emphasize it.

"Now you know," said Ginnie, and opened a copy of *Vogue* in front of her face. She kept it in this position till Selena had left the room, then put it back on top of the radio. She looked around the room, mentally rearranging furniture, throwing out table lamps, removing artificial flowers. In her opinion, it was an altogether hideous room—expensive but cheesy.

Suddenly, a male voice shouted from another part of the apartment, *"Eric? That you?"*

Ginnie guessed it was Selena's brother, whom she had never seen. She crossed her long legs, arranged the hem of her polo coat over her knees, and waited.

A young man wearing glasses and pajamas and no slippers lunged into the room with his mouth open. "Oh. I thought it was Eric, for Chrissake," he said. Without stopping, and with extremely poor posture, he continued across the room, cradling something close to his narrow chest. He sat down on the vacant end of the sofa. "I just cut my goddam finger," he said rather wildly. He looked at Ginnie as if he had expected her to be sitting there. "Ever cut your finger? Right down to the bone and all?" he asked. There was a real appeal in his noisy voice, as if Ginnie, by her

answer, could save him from some particularly isolating form of pioneering.

Ginnie stared at him. "Well, not right down to the
bone," she said, "but I've cut myself." He was the
funniest-looking boy, or man—it was hard to tell which
he was—she had ever seen. His hair was bed-di-
shevelled. He had a couple of days' growth of sparse,
blond beard. And he looked—well, goofy. "How did
you cut it?" she asked.

He was staring down, with his slack mouth ajar,
at his injured finger. "What?" he said.

"How did you cut it?"

"Goddam if *I* know," he said, his inflection implying that the answer to that question was hopelessly
obscure. "I was lookin' for something in the goddam
wastebasket and it was fulla razor blades."

"You Selena's brother?" Ginnie asked.

"Yeah. Christ, I'm bleedin' to death. Stick around.
I may need a goddam transfusion."

"Did you put anything on it?"

Selena's brother carried his wound slightly forward
from his chest and unveiled it for Ginnie's benefit.
"Just some goddam toilet paper," he said. "Stopsa
bleeding. Like when you cut yourself shaving." He
looked at Ginnie again. "Who are you?" he asked.
"Friend of the jerk's?"

"We're in the same class."

"Yeah? What's your name?"

"Virginia Mannox."

"You Ginnie?" he said, squinting at her through his
glasses. "You Ginnie Mannox?"

"Yes," said Ginnie, uncrossing her legs.

Selena's brother turned back to his finger, obviously
for him the true and only focal point in the room. "I

know your sister," he said dispassionately. "Goddam snob."

Ginnie arched her back. "*Who* is?"

"You heard me."

"She is *not* a snob!"

"The hell she's not," said Selena's brother.

"She is *not!*"

"The hell she's not. She's the queen. Queen of the goddam snobs."

Ginnie watched him left up and peer under the thick folds of toilet paper on his finger.

"You don't even *know* my sister."

"Hell I don't."

"What's her name? What's her first name?" Ginnie demanded.

"Joan. . . . Joan the Snob."

Ginnie was silent. "What's she look like?" she asked suddenly.

No answer.

"What's she look like?" Ginnie repeated.

"If she was half as good-looking as she *thinks* she is, she'd be goddam lucky," Selena's brother said.

This had the stature of an interesting answer, in Ginnie's secret opinion. "I never heard her mention *you*," she said.

"That worries me. That worries hell outa me."

"Anyway, she's engaged," Ginnie said, watching him. "She's gonna be married next month."

"Who to?" he asked, looking up.

Ginnie took full advantage of his having looked up. "Nobody *you* know."

He resumed picking at his own first-aid work. "I pity him," he said.

Ginnie snorted.

"It's still bleedin' like mad. Ya think I oughta put

[44]

something on it? What's good to put on it? Mercurochrome any good?"

"Iodine's better," Ginnie said. Then, feeling her
answer was too civil under the circumstances, she
added, "Mercurochrome's no good at *all* for that."

"Why not? What's the matter with it?"

"It just isn't any *good* for that stuff, that's all. Ya
need iodine."

He looked at Ginnie. "It stings a lot, though, doesn't
it?" he asked. "Doesn't it sting a helluva lot?"

"It *stings*," Ginnie said, "but it won't kill you or
anything."

Apparently without resenting Ginnie's tone, Selena's
brother turned back to his finger. "I don't like it when
it stings," he said.

"*No*body does."

He nodded in agreement. "Yeah," he said.

Ginnie watched him for a minute. "Stop touching
it," she said suddenly.

As though responding to an electric shock, Selena's
brother pulled back his uninjured hand. He sat up a
trifle straighter—or rather, slumped a trifle less. He
looked at some object on the other side of the room.
An almost dreamy expression came over his disorderly
features. He inserted the nail of his uninjured index
finger into the crevice between two front teeth and,
removing a food particle, turned to Ginnie. "Jeat jet?"
he asked.

"What?"

"Jeat lunch yet?"

Ginnie shook her head. "I'll eat when I get home,"
she said. "My mother always has lunch ready for me
when I get home."

"I got a half a chicken sandwich in my room. Ya
want it? I didn't touch it or anything."

"No, thank you. Really."

"You just played tennis, for Chrissake. Aren'tcha hungry?"

"It isn't that," said Ginnie, crossing her legs. "It's just that my mother always has lunch ready when I get home. She goes insane if I'm not hungry, I mean."

Selena's brother seemed to accept this explanation. At least, he nodded and looked away. But he turned back suddenly. "How 'bout a glassa milk?" he said.

"No, thanks. . . . Thank you, though."

Absently, he bent over and scratched his bare ankle. "What's the name of this guy she's marrying?" he asked.

"Joan, you mean?" said Ginnie. "Dick Heffner."

Selena's brother went on scratching his ankle.

"He's a lieutenant commander in the Navy," Ginnie said.

"Big deal."

Ginnie giggled. She watched him scratch his ankle till it was red. When he began to scratch off a minor skin eruption on his calf with his fingernail, she stopped watching.

"Where do you know Joan from?" she asked. "I never saw you at the house or anything."

"Never been at your goddam house."

Ginnie waited, but nothing led away from this statement. "Where'd you meet her, then?" she asked.

"Party," he said.

"At a party? When?"

"*I* don't know. Christmas, '42." From his breast pajama pocket he two-fingered out a cigarette that looked as though it had been slept on. "How 'bout throwing me those matches?" he said. Ginnie handed him a box of matches from the table beside her. He lit his cigarette without straightening out its curvature, then replaced the used match in the box. Tilting his head back, he slowly released an enormous quantity of smoke from his mouth and drew it up through his nostrils. He continued to smoke in this "French-inhale" style. Very probably, it was not part of the sofa vaudeville of a showoff but, rather, the private, exposed achievement of a young man who, at one time or another, might have tried shaving himself left-handed.

"Why's Joan a snob?" Ginnie asked.

"Why? Because she is. How the hell do I know why?"

"Yes, but I mean why do you say she is?"

He turned to her wearily. "Listen. I wrote her eight goddam letters. *Eight*. She didn't answer *one* of 'em."

Ginnie hesitated. "Well, maybe she was busy."

"Yeah. Busy. Busy as a little goddam beaver."

"Do you have to *swear* so much?" Ginnie asked.

"Goddam right I do."

Ginnie giggled. "How long did you know her, anyway?" she asked.

"Long enough."

"Well, I mean did you ever phone her up or anything? I mean didn't you ever phone her up or anything?"

"Naa."

"Well, my gosh. If you never phoned her up or any—"

"I couldn't, for Chrissake!"

"Why not?" said Ginnie.

"Wasn't *in* New York."

"Oh! Where were you?"

"Me? Ohio."

"Oh, were you in college?"

"Nope. Quit."

"Oh, were you in the Army?"

"Nope." With his cigarette hand, Selena's brother tapped the left side of his chest. "Ticker," he said.

"Your heart, ya mean?" Ginnie said. "What's the matter with it?"

"*I* don't know what the hell's the matter with it. I had rheumatic fever when I was a kid. Goddam pain in the—"

"Well, aren't you supposed to stop smoking? I mean aren't you supposed to not smoke and all? The doctor told my—"

"Aah, they tellya a lotta stuff," he said.

Ginnie briefly held her fire. Very briefly. "What were you doing in Ohio?" she asked.

"Me? Working in a goddam airplane factory."

"You were?" said Ginnie. "Did you like it?"

" 'Did you like it?' " he mimicked. "I loved it. I just *adore* airplanes. They're so *cute*."

Ginnie was much too involved now to feel affronted. "How long did you work there? In the airplane factory."

"*I* don't know, for Chrissake. Thirty-seven months." He stood up and walked over to the window. He looked down at the street, scratching his spine with his thumb. "Look at 'em," he said. "Goddam fools."

"Who?" said Ginnie.

"*I* don't know. Anybody."

"Your finger'll start bleeding more if you hold it *down* that way," Ginnie said.

He heard her. He put his left foot up on the window seat and rested his injured hand on the horizontal thigh. He continued to look down at the street. "They're all goin' over to the goddam draft board," he said. "We're gonna fight the Eskimos next. Know that?"

"The who?" said Ginnie.

"The *Eskimos*. . . . Open your ears, for Chrissake."

"Why the Eskimos?"

"*I* don't know why. How the hell should *I* know why? This time all the old guys're gonna go. Guys around sixty. Nobody can go unless they're around sixty," he said. "Just give 'em shorter hours is all. . . . Big deal."

"*You* wouldn't have to go, anyway," Ginnie said, without meaning anything but the truth, yet knowing before the statement was completely out that she was saying the wrong thing.

"I know," he said quickly, and took his foot down from the window seat. He raised the window slightly and snapped his cigarette streetward. Then he turned, finished at the window. "Hey. Do me a favor. When this guy comes, willya tell him I'll be ready in a coupla seconds? I just gotta shave is all. O.K.?"

Ginnie nodded.

"Ya want me to hurry Selena up or anything? She know you're here?"

"Oh, she knows I'm here," Ginnie said. "I'm in no hurry. Thank you."

Selena's brother nodded. Then he took a last, long look at his injured finger, as if to see whether it was in condition to make the trip back to his room.

"Why don't you put a Band-Aid on it? Don't you have any Band-Aid or anything?"

"Naa," he said. "Well. Take it easy." He wandered out of the room.

In a few seconds, he was back, bringing the sandwich half.

"Eat this," he said. "It's good."

"Really, I'm not at all—"

"*Take* it, for Chrissake. I didn't poison it or anything."

Ginnie accepted the sandwich half. "Well, thank you very much," she said.

"It's chicken," he said, standing over her, watching her. "Bought it last night in a goddam delicatessen."

"It looks very good."

"Well, *eat* it, then."

Ginnie took a bite.

"Good, huh?"

Ginnie swallowed with difficulty. "Very," she said.

Selena's brother nodded. He looked absently around the room, scratching the pit of his chest. "Well, I guess I better get dressed. . . . Jesus! There's the bell. Take it easy, now!" He was gone.

Left alone, Ginnie looked around, without getting up, for a good place to throw out or hide the sandwich. She heard someone coming through the foyer. She put the sandwich into her polo-coat pocket.

A young man in his early thirties, neither short nor tall, came into the room. His regular features, his short haircut, the cut of his suit, the pattern of his foulard necktie gave out no really final information. He might have been on the staff, or trying to get on the staff, of a news magazine. He might have just been in a play that closed in Philadelphia. He might have been with a law firm.

"Hello," he said, cordially, to Ginnie.

"Hello."

"Seen Franklin?" he asked.

"He's shaving. He told me to tell you to wait for him. He'll be right out."

"*Shaving.* Good heavens." The young man looked

at his wristwatch. He then sat down in a red damask chair, crossed his legs, and put his hands to his face. As if he were generally weary, or had just undergone some form of eyestrain, he rubbed his closed eyes with the tips of his extended fingers. "This has been the most horrible morning of my entire life," he said, removing his hands from his face. He spoke exclusively from the larynx, as if he were altogether too tired to put any diaphragm breath into his words.

"What happened?" Ginnie asked, looking at him.

"Oh. . . . It's too long a story. I never bore people I haven't known for at least a thousand years." He stared vaguely, discontentedly, in the direction of the windows. "But I shall never again consider myself even the *remote*st judge of human nature. You may quote me wildly on that."

"What happened?" Ginnie repeated.

"Oh, God. This person who's been sharing my apartment for months and months and months—I don't even want to talk about him. . . . This *writer*," he added with satisfaction, probably remembering a favorite anathema from a Hemingway novel.

"What'd he do?"

"*Frankly,* I'd just as soon not go into details," said the young man. He took a cigarette from his own pack, ignoring a transparent humidor on the table, and lit it with his own lighter. His hands were large. They looked neither strong nor competent nor sensitive. Yet he used them as if they had some not easily controllable aesthetic drive of their own. "I've made up my mind that I'm not even going to think about it. But I'm just so furious," he said. "I mean here's this awful little person from Al*toon*a, Pennsylvania—or *one* of those places. Apparently *starving* to death. I'm kind and *decent* enough—I'm the *original*

Good Samaritan—to *take* him into my apartment, this absolutely micro*scop*ic little apartment that I can hardly move around in myself. I introduce him to *all* my friends. Let him clutter up the *whole* apartment with his horrible manuscript papers, and cigarette butts, and *radishes,* and whatnot. *In*troduce him to every theatrical producer in New York. *Haul* his filthy shirts back and forth from the laundry. And on top of it *all*—" The young man broke off. "And the result of all my kindness and *decency*," he went on, "is that he walks out of the house at five or six in the morning—without so much as leaving a *note* behind —taking with him anything and everything he can lay his filthy, dirty hands on." He paused to drag on his cigarette, and exhaled the smoke in a thin, sibilant stream from his mouth. "I don't want to talk about it. I really don't." He looked over at Ginnie. "I love your coat," he said, already out of his chair. He crossed over and took the lapel of Ginnie's polo coat between his fingers. "It's lovely. It's the first really *good* camel's hair I've seen since the war. May I ask where you got it?"

"My mother brought it back from Nassau."

The young man nodded thoughtfully and backed off toward his chair. "It's one of the few places where you can get really *good* camel's hair." He sat down. "Was she there long?"

"What?" said Ginnie.

"Was your mother there long? The reason I ask is *my* mother was down in December. And part of January. *Us*ually I go down with her, but this has been such a messy year I simply couldn't get away."

"She was down in February," Ginnie said.

"Grand. Where did she stay? Do you know?"

"With my aunt."

He nodded. "May I ask your name? You're a friend of Franklin's sister, I take it?"

"We're in the same class," Ginnie said, answering only his second question.

"You're not the famous *Maxine* that Selena talks about, are you?"

"No," Ginnie said.

The young man suddenly began brushing the cuffs of his trousers with the flat of his hand. "I am *dog hairs* from head to foot," he said. "Mother went to Washington over the weekend and parked her beast in *my* apartment. It's really quite sweet. But such nasty habits. Do you have a dog?"

"No."

"Actually, I think it's cruel to keep them in the city." He stopped brushing, sat back, and looked at his wristwatch again. "I have *never* known that boy to be on time. We're going to see Cocteau's 'Beauty and the Beast' and it's the *one* film where you really *should* get there on time. I mean if you don't, the whole *charm* of it is gone. Have you seen it?"

"No."

"Oh, you must! I've seen it eight times. It's absolutely pure genius," he said. "I've been *try*ing to get Franklin to see it for months." He shook his head hopelessly. "His taste. During the war, we both worked at the same horrible place, and that boy would in*sist* on dragging me to the most impossible pictures in the world. We saw gangster pictures, Western pictures, *musicals*—"

"Did you work in the airplane factory, too?" Ginnie asked.

"God, yes. For years and years and years. Let's not talk about it, please."

"You have a bad heart, too?"

"Heavens, no. Knock wood." He rapped the arm of his chair twice. "I have the constitution of—"

As Selena entered the room, Ginnie stood up quickly and went to meet her halfway. Selena had changed from her shorts to a dress, a fact that ordinarily would have annoyed Ginnie.

"I'm sorry to've kept you waiting," Selena said insincerely, "but I had to wait for Mother to wake up. . . . Hello, Eric."

"Hello, hello!"

"I don't want the money anyway," Ginnie said, keeping her voice down so that she was heard only by Selena.

"What?"

"I've been thinking. I mean you bring the tennis balls and all, all the time. I forgot about that."

"But you said that because I didn't have to pay for them—"

"Walk me to the door," Ginnie said, leading the way, without saying goodbye to Eric.

"But I thought you said you were going to the movies tonight and you needed the money and all!" Selena said in the foyer.

"I'm too tired," Ginnie said. She bent over and picked up her tennis paraphernalia. "Listen. I'll give you a ring after dinner. Are you doing anything special tonight? Maybe I can come over."

Selena stared and said, "O.K."

Ginnie opened the front door and walked to the elevator. She rang the bell. "I met your brother," she said.

"You did? Isn't he a character?"

"What's he do, anyway?" Ginnie asked casually. "Does he work or something?"

"He just quit. Daddy wants him to go back to college, but he won't go."

"Why won't he?"

"I don't know. He says he's too old and all."

"How old is he?"

"I don't know. Twenty-four."

The elevator doors opened. "I'll call you later!" Ginnie said.

Outside the building, she started to walk west to Lexington to catch the bus. Between Third and Lexington, she reached into her coat pocket for her purse and found the sandwich half. She took it out and started to bring her arm down, to drop the sandwich into the street, but instead she put it back into her pocket. A few years before, it had taken her three days to dispose of the Easter chick she had found dead on the sawdust in the bottom of her wastebasket.

The Laughing Man

In 1928, when I was nine, I belonged, with maximum *esprit de corps,* to an organization known as the Comanche Club. Every schoolday afternoon at three o'clock, twenty-five of us Comanches were picked up by our Chief outside the boys' exit of P. S. 165, on 109th Street near Amsterdam Avenue. We then pushed and punched our way into the Chief's reconverted commercial bus, and he drove us (according to his financial arrangement with our parents) over to Central Park. The rest of the afternoon, weather permitting, we played football or soccer or baseball, depending (very loosely) on the season. Rainy afternoons, the Chief invariably took us either to the Museum of Natural History or to the Metropolitan Museum of Art.

Saturdays and most national holidays, the Chief picked us up early in the morning at our various apartment houses and, in his condemned-looking bus, drove us out of Manhattan into the comparatively wide open spaces of Van Cortlandt Park or the Palisades. If we had straight athletics on our minds, we went to Van Cortlandt, where the playing fields were regulation size and where the opposing team didn't include a baby carriage or an irate old lady with a cane. If our Comanche hearts were set on camping, we went over to the Palisades and roughed it. (I remember getting lost one Saturday somewhere on that tricky stretch of terrain between the Linit sign and the site of the western end of the George Washington Bridge. I kept my head, though. I just sat down in the majestic shadow of a giant billboard and, however tearfully, opened my lunchbox for business, semi-confident that the Chief would find me. The Chief always found us.)

In his hours of liberation from the Comanches, the Chief was John Gedsudski, of Staten Island. He was an extremely shy, gentle young man of twenty-two or -three, a law student at N.Y.U., and altogether a very memorable person. I won't attempt to assemble his many achievements and virtues here. Just in passing, he was an Eagle Scout, an almost-All-America tackle of 1926, and it was known that he had been most cordially invited to try out for the New York Giants' baseball team. He was an impartial and unexcitable umpire at all our bedlam sporting events, a master fire builder and extinguisher, and an expert, uncontemptuous first-aid man. Every one of us, from the smallest hoodlum to the biggest, loved and respected him.

The Chief's physical appearance in 1928 is still clear in my mind. If wishes were inches, all of us Comanches would have had him a giant in no time. The way things go, though, he was a stocky five three or four—no more than that. His hair was blue-black, his hair-line extremely low, his nose was large and fleshy, and his torso was just about as long as his legs were. In his leather windbreaker, his shoulders were powerful, but narrow and sloping. At the time, however, it seemed to me that in the Chief all the most photogenic features of Buck Jones, Ken Maynard, and Tom Mix had been smoothly amalgamated.

Every afternoon, when it got dark enough for a losing team to have an excuse for missing a number of infield popups or end-zone passes, we Comanches relied heavily and selfishly on the Chief's talent for storytelling. By that hour, we were usually an overheated, irritable bunch, and we fought each other—either with our fists or our shrill voices—for the seats in the bus nearest the Chief. (The bus had two parallel rows of straw seats. The left row had three extra seats—the best in the bus—that extended as far forward as the driver's profile.) The Chief climbed into the bus only after we had settled down. Then he straddled his driver's seat backward and, in his reedy but modulated tenor voice, gave us the new installment of "The Laughing Man." Once he started narrating, our interest never flagged. "The Laughing Man" was just the right story for a Comanche. It may even have had classic dimensions. It was a story that tended to sprawl all over the place, and yet it remained essentially portable. You could always take it home with you and reflect on it while sitting, say, in the outgoing water in the bathtub.

The only son of a wealthy missionary couple, the Laughing Man was kidnapped in infancy by Chinese bandits. When the wealthy missionary couple refused (from a religious conviction) to pay the ransom for their son, the bandits, signally piqued, placed the little fellow's head in a carpenter's vise and gave the appropriate lever several turns to the right. The subject of this unique experience grew into manhood with a hairless, pecan-shaped head and a face that featured, instead of a mouth, an enormous oval cavity below the nose. The nose itself consisted of two flesh-sealed nostrils. In consequence, when the Laughing Man breathed, the hideous, mirthless gap below his nose dilated and contracted like (as *I* see it) some sort of monstrous vacuole. (The Chief demonstrated, rather than explained, the Laughing Man's respiration method.) Strangers fainted dead away at the sight of the Laughing Man's horrible face. Acquaintances shunned him. Curiously enough, though, the bandits let him hang around their headquarters—as long as he kept his face covered with a pale-red gossamer mask made out of poppy petals. The mask not only spared the bandits the sight of their foster son's face, it also kept them sensible of his whereabouts; under the circumstances, he reeked of opium.

Every morning, in his extreme loneliness, the Laughing Man stole off (he was as graceful on his feet as a cat) to the dense forest surrounding the bandits' hideout. There he befriended any number and species of animals: dogs, white mice, eagles, lions, boa constrictors, wolves. Moreover, he removed his mask and spoke to them, softly, melodiously, in their own tongues. They did not think him ugly.

(It took the Chief a couple of months to get that far into the story. From there on in, he got more and more high-handed with his installments, entirely to the satisfaction of the Comanches.)

The Laughing Man was one for keeping an ear to the ground, and in no time at all he had picked up the bandits' most valuable trade secrets. He didn't think much of them, though, and briskly set up his own, more effective system. On a rather small scale at first, he began to free-lance around the Chinese countryside, robbing, highjacking, murdering when absolutely necessary. Soon his ingenious criminal methods, coupled with his singular love of fair play, found him a warm place in the nation's heart. Strangely enough, his foster parents (the bandits who had originally turned his head toward crime) were about the last to get wind of his achievements. When they did, they were insanely jealous. They all single-filed past the Laughing Man's bed one night, thinking they had successfully doped him into a deep sleep, and stabbed at the figure under the covers with their machetes. The victim turned out to be the bandit chief's mother—an unpleasant, haggling sort of person. The event only whetted the bandits' taste for the Laughing Man's blood, and finally he was obliged to lock up the whole bunch of them in a deep but pleasantly decorated mausoleum. They escaped from time to time and gave him a certain amount of annoyance, but he refused to kill them. (There was a compassionate side to the Laughing Man's character that just about drove me crazy.)

Soon the Laughing Man was regularly crossing the Chinese border into Paris, France, where he enjoyed flaunting his high but modest genius in the face of Marcel Dufarge, the internationally famous detective and witty consumptive. Dufarge and his daughter (an exquisite girl, though something of a transvestite) became the Laughing Man's bitterest enemies. Time and again, they tried leading the Laughing Man up the garden path. For sheer sport, the Laughing Man usually went halfway with them, then vanished, often leaving no even faintly credible indication of his escape method. Just now and then he posted an incisive little farewell note in the Paris sewerage system, and it was delivered promptly to Dufarge's boot.

The Dufarges spent an enormous amount of time sloshing around in the Paris sewers.

Soon the Laughing Man had amassed the largest personal fortune in the world. Most of it he contributed anonymously to the monks of a local monastery—humble ascetics who had dedicated their lives to raising German police dogs. What was left of his fortune, the Laughing Man converted into diamonds, which he lowered casually, in emerald vaults, into the Black Sea. His personal wants were few. He subsisted exclusively on rice and eagles' blood, in a tiny cottage with an underground gymnasium and shooting range, on the stormy coast of Tibet. Four blindly loyal confederates lived with him: a glib timber wolf named Black Wing, a lovable dwarf named Omba, a giant Mongolian named Hong, whose tongue had been burned out by white men, and a gorgeous Eurasian girl, who, out of unrequited love for the Laughing Man and deep concern for his personal safety, sometimes had a pretty sticky attitude toward crime. The Laughing Man issued his orders to the crew through a black silk screen. Not even Omba, the lovable dwarf, was permitted to see his face.

I'm not saying I will, but I could go on for hours escorting the reader—forcibly, if necessary—back and forth across the Paris-Chinese border. I happen to regard the Laughing Man as some kind of super-distinguished ancestor of mine—a sort of Robert E. Lee, say, with the ascribed virtues held under water or blood. And this illusion is only a moderate one compared to the one I had in 1928, when I regarded myself not only as the Laughing Man's direct descendant but as his only legitimate living one. I was not even my parents' son in 1928 but a devilishly smooth impostor, awaiting their slightest blunder as an excuse to move in—preferably without violence, but not necessarily—to assert my true identity. As a precaution against breaking my bogus mother's heart, I planned to take her into my underworld employ in some undefined but appropriately regal capacity. But the *main* thing I had to do in 1928 was watch my step. Play along with the farce. Brush my teeth. Comb my hair. At all costs, stifle my natural hideous laughter.

Actually, I was not the only legitimate living descendant of the Laughing Man. There were twenty-five Comanches in the Club, or twenty-five legitimate living descendants of the Laughing Man—all of us circulating ominously, and incognito, throughout the city, sizing up elevator operators as potential archenemies, whispering side-of-the-mouth but fluent orders into the ears of cocker spaniels, drawing beads, with index fingers, on the foreheads of arithmetic teachers. And always waiting, waiting for a decent chance to strike terror and admiration in the nearest mediocre heart.

One afternoon in February, just after Comanche baseball season had opened, I observed a new fixture in the Chief's bus. Above the rear-view mirror over the windshield, there was a small, framed photograph of a girl dressed in academic cap and gown. It seemed to me that a girl's picture clashed with the general men-only décor of the bus, and I bluntly asked the Chief who she was. He hedged at first, but finally admitted that she was a girl. I asked him what her name was. He answered unforthrightly, "Mary Hudson." I asked him if she was in the movies or something. He said no, that she used to go to Wellesley College. He added, on some slow-processed afterthought, that Wellesley College was a very high-

class college. I asked him what he had her picture in
the *bus* for, though. He shrugged slightly, as much as
to imply, it seemed to me, that the picture had more
or less been planted on him.

During the next couple of weeks, the picture—
however forcibly or accidentally it had been planted
on the Chief—was not removed from the bus. It didn't
go out with the Baby Ruth wrappers and the fallen
licorice whips. However, we Comanches got used to
it. It gradually took on the unarresting personality of
a speedometer.

But one day as we were on our way to the Park,
the Chief pulled the bus over to a curb on Fifth
Avenue in the Sixties, a good half mile past our baseball field. Some twenty back-seat drivers at once demanded an explanation, but the Chief gave none. Instead, he simply got into his story-telling position and
swung prematurely into a fresh installment of "The
Laughing Man." He had scarcely begun, however, when
someone tapped on the bus door. The Chief's re-
flexes were geared high that day. He literally flung
himself around in his seat, yanked the operating
handle of the door, and a girl in a beaver coat climbed
into the bus.

Offhand, I can remember seeing just three girls in
my life who struck me as having unclassifiably great
beauty at first sight. One was a thin girl in a black
bathing suit who was having a lot of trouble putting
up an orange umbrella at Jones Beach, circa 1936.
The second was a girl aboard a Caribbean cruise ship
in 1939, who threw her cigarette lighter at a porpoise.
And the third was the Chief's girl, Mary Hudson.

"Am I very late?" she asked the Chief, smiling at
him.

She might just as well have asked if she was ugly.

"No!" the Chief said. A trifle wildly, he looked at the Comanches near his seat and signalled the row to give way. Mary Hudson sat down between me and a boy named Edgar something, whose uncle's best friend was a bootlegger. We gave her all the room in the world. Then the bus started off with a peculiar, amateur-like lurch. The Comanches, to the last man, were silent.

On the way back to our regular parking place, Mary Hudson leaned forward in her seat and gave the Chief an enthusiastic account of the trains she had missed and the train she hadn't missed; she lived in Douglaston, Long Island. The Chief was very nervous. He didn't just fail to contribute any talk of his own; he could hardly listen to hers. The gearshift knob came off in his hand, I remember.

When we got out of the bus, Mary Hudson stuck right with us. I'm sure that by the time we reached the baseball field there was on every Comanche's face a some-girls-just-don't-know-when-to-go-home look. And to really top things off, when another Comanche and I were flipping a coin to decide which team would take the field first, Mary Hudson wistfully expressed a desire to join the game. The response to this couldn't have been more clean-cut. Where before we Comanches had simply stared at her femaleness, we now glared at it. She smiled back at us. It was a shade disconcerting. Then the Chief took over, revealing what had formerly been a well-concealed flair for incompetence. He took Mary Hudson aside, just out of earshot of the Comanches, and seemed to address her solemnly, rationally. At length, Mary Hudson interrupted him, and her voice was perfectly audible to the Comanches. "But I *do*," she said. "I do, too, want to play!" The Chief nodded and tried again. He pointed in the direction of the infield, which was soggy and pitted. He picked up a regulation bat and demonstrated its weight. "I don't care," Mary Hudson said distinctly, "I came all the way to New York—to the dentist and everything—and I'm gonna play." The Chief nodded again but gave up. He walked cautiously over to home plate, where the Braves and the Warriors, the two Comanche teams, were waiting, and looked at me. I was captain of the Warriors. He mentioned the name of my regular center fielder, who was home sick, and suggested that Mary Hudson take his place. I said I didn't need a center fielder. The Chief asked me what the hell did I mean I didn't need a center fielder. I was shocked. It was the first time I had heard the Chief swear. What's more, I could feel Mary Hudson smiling at me. For poise, I picked up a stone and threw it at a tree.

We took the field first. No business went out to center field the first inning. From my position on first base, I glanced behind me now and then. Each time I did, Mary Hudson waved gaily to me. She was wearing a catcher's mitt, her own adamant choice. It was a horrible sight.

Mary Hudson batted ninth on the Warriors' lineup. When I informed her of this arrangement, she made a little face and said, "Well, hurry *up*, then." And as a matter of fact we did seem to hurry up. She got to bat in the first inning. She took off her beaver coat —and her catcher's mitt—for the occasion and advanced to the plate in a dark-brown dress. When I gave her a bat, she asked me why it was so *heavy*. The Chief left his umpire's position behind the pitcher and came forward anxiously. He told Mary Hudson to rest the end of her bat on her right shoulder. "I am," she said. He told her not to choke the bat too tightly. "I'm not," she said. He told her to keep her eye right on the ball. "I will," she said. "Get outa the *way*." She swung mightily at the first ball pitched to her and hit it over the left fielder's head. It was good for an ordinary double, but Mary Hudson got to third on it—standing up.

When my astonishment had worn off, and then my awe, and then my delight, I looked over at the Chief. He didn't so much seem to be standing behind the pitcher as floating over him. He was a completely happy man. Over on third base, Mary Hudson waved to me. I waved back. I couldn't have stopped myself, even if I'd wanted to. Her stickwork aside, she happened to be a girl who knew how to wave to somebody from third base.

The rest of the game, she got on base every time she came to bat. For some reason, she seemed to hate *first* base; there was no holding her there. At least three times, she stole second.

Her fielding couldn't have been worse, but we were piling up too many runs to take serious notice of it. I think it would have improved if she'd gone after flies with almost anything except a catcher's mitt. She wouldn't take it off, though. She said it was cute.

The next month or so, she played baseball with the Comanches a couple of times a week (whenever she had an appointment with her dentist, apparently). Some afternoons she met the bus on time, some afternoons she was late. Sometimes she talked a blue streak in the bus, sometimes she just sat and smoked her Herbert Tareyton cigarettes (cork-tipped). When you sat next to her in the bus, she smelled of a wonderful perfume.

One wintry day in April, after making his usual three

o'clock pickup at 109th and Amsterdam, the Chief turned the loaded bus east at 110th Street and cruised routinely down Fifth Avenue. But his hair was combed wet, he had on his overcoat instead of his leather windbreaker, and I reasonably surmised that Mary Hudson was scheduled to join us. When we zipped past our usual entrance to the Park, I was sure of it. The Chief parked the bus on the corner in the Sixties appropriate to the occasion. Then, to kill time painlessly for the Comanches, he straddled his seat backward and released a new installment of "The Laughing Man." I remember the installment to the last detail, and I must outline it briefly.

A flux of circumstances delivered the Laughing Man's best friend, his timber wolf, Black Wing, into a physical and intellectual trap set by the Dufarges. The Dufarges, aware of the Laughing Man's high sense of loyalty, offered him Black Wing's freedom in exchange for his own. In the best faith in the world, the Laughing Man agreed to these terms. (Some of the minor mechanics of his genius were often subject to mysterious little breakdowns.) It was arranged for the Laughing Man to meet the Dufarges at midnight in a designated section of the dense forest surrounding Paris, and there, by moonlight, Black Wing would be set free. However, the Dufarges had no intention of liberating Black Wing, whom they feared and loathed. On the night of the transaction, they leashed a stand-in timber wolf for Black Wing, first dyeing its left hind foot snow white, to look like Black Wing's.

But there were two things the Dufarges hadn't counted on: the Laughing Man's sentimentality and his command of the timber-wolf language. As soon as he had allowed Dufarge's daughter to tie him with barbed wire to a tree, the Laughing Man felt called upon to raise his beautiful, melodious voice in a few words of farewell to his supposed old friend. The stand-in, a few moonlit yards away, was impressed by the stranger's command of the language and listened politely for a moment to the last-minute advice, personal and professional, that the Laughing Man was giving out. At length, though, the stand-in grew impatient and began shifting his weight from paw to paw. Abruptly, and rather unpleasantly, he interrupted the Laughing Man with the information that, in the first place, his name wasn't Dark Wing or Black Wing or Gray Legs or any of that business, it was Armand, and, in the second place, he'd never been to China in his life and hadn't the slightest intention of going there.

Properly infuriated, the Laughing Man pushed off his mask with his tongue and confronted the Dufarges with his naked face by moonlight. Mlle. Dufarge responded by passing out cold. Her father was luckier. By chance, he was having one of his coughing spells at the moment and thereby missed the lethal unveiling. When his coughing spell was over and he saw his daughter stretched out supine on the moonlit ground, Dufarge put two and two together. Shielding his eyes with his hand, he fired the full clip in his automatic toward the sound of the Laughing Man's heavy, sibilant breathing.

The installment ended there.

The Chief took his dollar Ingersoll out of his watch pocket, looked at it, then swung around in his seat and started up the motor. I checked my own watch. It was almost four-thirty. As the bus moved forward, I asked the Chief if he wasn't going to wait for Mary Hudson. He didn't answer me, and before I could repeat my question, he tilted back his head and addressed all of us: "Let's have a little quiet in this damn bus." Whatever else it may have been, the order was basically unsensible. The bus had been, and was, very quiet. Almost everybody was thinking about the spot the Laughing Man had been left in. We were long past *worrying* about him—we had too much confidence in him for that—but we were never past accepting his most perilous moments quietly.

In the third or fourth inning of our ball game that afternoon, I spotted Mary Hudson from first base. She was sitting on a bench about a hundred yards to my left, sandwiched between two nursemaids with baby carriages. She had on her beaver coat, she was smoking a cigarette, and she seemed to be looking in the direction of our game. I got excited about my discovery and yelled the information over to the Chief, behind the pitcher. He hurried over to me, not quite running. "Where?" he asked me. I pointed again. He stared for a moment in the right direction, then said he'd be back in a minute and left the field. He left it slowly, opening his overcoat and putting his hands in the hip pockets of his trousers. I sat down on first base and watched. By the time the Chief reached Mary Hudson, his overcoat was buttoned again and his hands were down at his sides.

He stood over her for about five minutes, apparently talking to her. Then Mary Hudson stood up, and the two of them walked toward the baseball field. They didn't talk as they walked, or look at each other. When they reached the field, the Chief took his position behind the pitcher. I yelled over to him. "Isn't she gonna play?" He told me to cover my sack. I covered my sack and watched Mary Hudson. She walked slowly behind the plate, with her hands in the pockets of her beaver coat, and finally sat down on a misplaced players' bench just beyond third base. She lit another cigarette and crossed her legs.

When the Warriors were at bat, I went over to her bench and asked her if she felt like playing left field. She shook her head. I asked her if she had a cold. She shook her head again. I told her I didn't have anybody in left field. I told her I had a guy playing center field *and* left field. There was no response at all to this information. I tossed my first-baseman's mitt up in the air and tried to have it land on my head, but it fell in a mud puddle. I wiped it off on my trousers and asked Mary Hudson if she wanted to come up to my house for dinner sometime. I told her the Chief came up a lot. "Leave me alone," she said. "Just please leave me alone." I stared at her, then walked off in the direction of the Warriors' bench, taking a tangerine out of my pocket and tossing it up in the air. About midway along the third-base foul line, I turned around and started to walk backwards, looking at Mary Hudson and holding on to my tangerine. I had no idea what was going on between the Chief and Mary Hudson (and still haven't, in any but a fairly low, intuitive sense), but nonetheless, I couldn't have been more certain that Mary Hudson had permanently dropped out of the Comanche lineup. It was the kind of whole certainty, however independent of the sum of its facts, that can make walking backwards more than normally hazardous, and I bumped smack into a baby carriage.

After another inning, the light got bad for fielding. The game was called, and we started picking up all the equipment. The last good look I had at Mary Hudson, she was over near third base crying. The Chief had hold of the sleeve of her beaver coat, but she got away from him. She ran off the field onto the cement path and kept running till I couldn't see her any more.

The Chief didn't go after her. He just stood watching her disappear. Then he turned around and walked down to home plate and picked up our two bats; we always left the bats for him to carry. I went over to him and asked if he and Mary Hudson had had a fight. He told me to tuck my shirt in.

Just as always, we Comanches ran the last few hundred feet to the place where the bus was parked, yelling, shoving, trying out strangleholds on each other, but all of us alive to the fact that it was again time for "The Laughing Man." Racing across Fifth Avenue, somebody dropped his extra or discarded sweater, and I tripped over it and went sprawling. I finished the charge to the bus, but the best seats were taken by that time and I had to sit down in the middle of the bus. Annoyed at the arrangement, I gave the boy sitting on my right a poke in the ribs with my elbow, then faced around and watched the Chief cross over Fifth. It was not yet dark out, but a five-fifteen dimness had set in. The Chief crossed the street with his coat collar up, the bats under his left arm, and his concentration on the street. His black hair, which had been combed wet earlier in the day, was dry now and blowing. I remember wishing the Chief had gloves.

The bus, as usual, was quiet when he climbed in— as proportionately quiet, at any rate, as a theatre with dimming house lights. Conversations were finished in a hurried whisper or shut off completely. Nonetheless, the first thing the Chief said to us was "All right, let's cut out the noise, or no story." In an instant, an unconditional silence filled the bus, cutting off from the Chief any alternative but to take up his narrating position. When he had done so, he took out a handkerchief and methodically blew his nose, one nostril at a time. We watched him with patience and even a certain amount of spectator's interest. When he had finished with his handkerchief, he folded it neatly in quarters and replaced it in his pocket. He then gave us the new installment of "The Laughing Man." From start to finish, it lasted no longer than five minutes.

Four of Dufarge's bullets struck the Laughing Man, two of them through the heart. When Dufarge, who was still shielding his eyes against the sight of the Laughing Man's face, heard a queer exhalation of agony from the direction of the target, he was overjoyed. His black heart beating wildly, he rushed over to his unconscious daughter and brought her to. The pair of them, beside themselves with delight and coward's courage, now dared to look up at the Laughing Man. His head was bowed as in death, his chin resting on his bloody chest. Slowly, greedily, father and daughter came forward to inspect their spoils. Quite a surprise was in store for them. The Laughing Man, far from dead, was busy contracting his stomach muscles in a secret manner. As the Dufarges came into range, he suddenly raised his face, gave a terrible laugh, and neatly, even fastidiously, regurgitated all four bullets. The impact of this feat on the Dufarges was so acute that their hearts literally burst, and they dropped dead at the Laughing Man's feet. (If the installment was going to be a short one *any*way, it could have ended there; the Comanches could have managed to rationalize the sudden death of the Dufarges. But it didn't end there.) Day after day, the Laughing Man continued to stand lashed to the tree with barbed wire, the Dufarges decomposing at his feet. Bleeding profusely and cut off from his supply of eagles' blood, he had never been closer to death. One day, however, in a hoarse but eloquent voice, he appealed for help to the animals of the forest. He summoned them to fetch Omba, the lovable dwarf. And they did. But it was a long trip back and forth across the Paris-Chinese border, and by the time Omba arrived on the scene with a medical kit and a fresh supply of eagles' blood, the Laughing Man was in a coma. Omba's very first act of mercy was to retrieve his master's mask, which had blown up against Mlle. Dufarge's vermin-infested torso. He placed it respectfully over the hideous features, then proceeded to dress the wounds.

When the Laughing Man's small eyes finally opened, Omba eagerly raised the vial of eagles' blood up to the mask. But the Laughing Man didn't drink from it. Instead, he weakly pronounced his beloved Black Wing's name. Omba bowed his own slightly distorted head and revealed to his master that the Dufarges had killed Black Wing. A peculiar and heart-rending gasp of final sorrow came from the Laughing Man. He reached out wanly for the vial of eagles' blood and crushed it in his hand. What little blood he had left trickled thinly down his wrist. He ordered Omba to look away, and, sobbing, Omba obeyed him. The Laughing Man's last act, before turning his face to the bloodstained ground, was to pull off his mask.

The story ended there, of course. (Never to be revived.) The Chief started up the bus. Across the aisle from me, Billy Walsh, who was the youngest of all the Comanches, burst into tears. None of us told him to shut up. As for me, I remember my knees were shaking.

A few minutes later, when I stepped out of the Chief's bus, the first thing I chanced to see was a piece of red tissue paper flapping in the wind against the base of a lamppost. It looked like someone's poppy-petal mask. I arrived home with my teeth chattering uncontrollably and was told to go right straight to bed.

Down at the Dinghy

IT WAS a little after four o'clock on an Indian Summer afternoon. Some fifteen or twenty times since noon, Sandra, the maid, had come away from the lake-front window in the kitchen with her mouth set tight. This time as she came away, she absently untied and re-tied her apron strings, taking up what little slack her enormous waistline allowed. Then she went back to the enamel table and lowered her freshly uniformed body into the seat opposite Mrs. Snell. Mrs. Snell having finished the cleaning and ironing was having her customary cup of tea before walking down the road to the bus stop. Mrs. Snell had her hat on. It was the same interesting, black felt headpiece she had worn, not just all summer, but for the past three summers—through record heat waves, through change of life, over scores of ironing boards, over the helms of dozens of vacuum cleaners. The Hattie Carnegie label was still inside it, faded but (it might be said) unbowed.

"I'm not gonna worry about it," Sandra announced, for the fifth or sixth time, addressing herself as much as Mrs. Snell. "I made up my mind I'm not gonna worry about it. What *for?*"

"That's right," said Mrs. Snell. "*I* wouldn't. I really wouldn't. Reach me my bag, dear."

A leather handbag, extremely worn, but with a label inside it as impressive as the one inside Mrs. Snell's hat, lay on the pantry. Sandra was able to reach it without standing up. She handed it across the table to Mrs. Snell, who opened it and took out a pack of mentholated cigarettes and a folder of Stork Club matches.

Mrs. Snell lit a cigarette, then brought her teacup to her lips, but immediately set it down in its saucer. "If this don't hurry up and cool off, I'm gonna miss my bus." She looked over at Sandra, who was staring, oppressedly, in the general direction of the copper sauce-pans lined against the wall. "Stop *worryin'* about it," Mrs. Snell ordered. "What good's it gonna do to worry about it? Either he tells her or he don't. That's all. What good's *worryin'* gonna do?"

"I'm not *worryin'* about it," Sandra responded. "The last thing I'm gonna do is *worry* about it. Only, it drives ya loony, the way that kid goes pussyfootin' all around the house. Ya can't *hear* him, ya know. I mean nobody can *hear* him, ya know. Just the other day I was shellin' beans—right at this here table— and I almost stepped on his *hand*. He was sittin' right under the table."

"Well. I wouldn't worry about it."

"I mean ya gotta weigh every word ya say around him," Sandra said. "It drives ya loony."

"I *still* can't drink this," Mrs. Snell said. ". . . That's terrible. When ya gotta weigh every word ya say and all."

"It drives ya loony! I mean it. Half the time I'm half loony." Sandra brushed some imaginary crumbs off her lap, and snorted. "A four-year-old kid!"

"He's kind of a good-lookin' kid," said Mrs. Snell. "Them big brown eyes and all."

Sandra snorted again. "He's gonna have a nose just like the father." She raised her cup and drank from it without any difficulty. "*I* don't know what they wanna stay up here all October for," she said malcontentedly, lowering her cup. "I mean none of 'em even go any-wheres *near* the water now. *She* don't go in, *he* don't go in, the *kid* don't go in. *No*body goes in now. They don't even take that crazy boat out no more. I don't know what they threw good money away on it for."

"I don't know how you can drink yours. I can't even drink mine."

Sandra stared rancorously at the opposite wall. "I'll be so gladda get backa the city. I'm not foolin'. I hate this crazy place." She gave Mrs. Snell a hostile glance. "It's all right for *you*, you live here all year round. You got your social life here and all. You don't care."

"I'm gonna drink this if it kills me," Mrs. Snell said, looking at the clock over the electric stove.

"What would *you* do if you were in my shoes?" Sandra asked abruptly. "I mean what would you do? Tella truth."

This was the sort of question Mrs. Snell slipped into as if it were an ermine coat. She at once let go her teacup. "Well, in the *first* place," she said, "I wouldn't *worry* about it. What *I'd* do, I'd look around for another—"

"I'm not *worried* about it," Sandra interrupted.

"I know that, but what *I'd* do, I'd just get me—"

The swinging door opened from the dining room

and Boo Boo Tannenbaum, the lady of the house, came into the kitchen. She was a small, almost hipless girl of twenty-five, with styleless, colorless, brittle hair pushed back behind her ears, which were very large. She was dressed in knee-length jeans, a black turtleneck pullover, and socks and loafers. Her joke of a name aside, her general unprettiness aside, she was—in terms of permanently memorable, immoderately perceptive, small-area faces—a stunning and final girl. She went directly to the refrigerator and opened it. As she peered inside, with her legs apart and her hands on her knees, she whistled, unmelodically, through her teeth, keeping time with a little uninhibited, pendulum action of her rear end. Sandra and Mrs. Snell were silent. Mrs. Snell put out her cigarette, unhurriedly.

"Sandra . . ."

"Yes, ma'am?" Sandra looked alertly past Mrs. Snell's hat.

"Aren't there any more pickles? I want to bring him a pickle."

"He et 'em," Sandra reported intelligently. "He et 'em before he went to bed last night. There was only two left."

"Oh. Well, I'll get some when I go to the station. I thought maybe I could lure him out of that boat." Boo Boo shut the refrigerator door and walked over to look out of the lake-front window. "Do we need anything else?" she asked, from the window.

"Just bread."

"I left your check on the hall table, Mrs. Snell. Thank you."

"O.K.," said Mrs. Snell. "I hear Lionel's supposeta be runnin' away." She gave a short laugh.

"Certainly looks that way," Boo Boo said, and slid her hands into her hip pockets.

"At least he don't run very *far* away," Mrs. Snell said, giving another short laugh.

At the window, Boo Boo changed her position slightly, so that her back wasn't directly to the two women at the table. "No," she said, and pushed back some hair behind her ear. She added, purely informatively: "He's been hitting the road regularly since he was two. But never very hard. I think the farthest he ever got—in the city, at least—was to the Mall in Central Park. Just a couple of blocks from home. The least far—or nearest—he ever got was to the front door of our building. He stuck around to say goodbye to his father."

Both women at the table laughed.

"The Mall's where they all go skatin' in New York," Sandra said very sociably to Mrs. Snell. "The kids and all."

"Oh!" said Mrs. Snell.

"He was only three. It was just last year," Boo Boo said, taking out a pack of cigarettes and a folder of matches from a side pocket in her jeans. She lit a cigarette, while the two women spiritedly watched her. "Big excitement. We had the whole police force out looking for him."

"They find him?" said Mrs. Snell.

"Sure they found him!" said Sandra with contempt. "Wuddaya *think*?"

"They found him at a quarter past eleven at night, in the middle of—my God, February, I think. Not a child in the park. Just muggers, I guess, and an assortment of roaming degenerates. He was sitting on the floor of the bandstand, rolling a marble back and forth along a crack. Half-frozen to death and look-ing—"

"Holy Mackerel!" said Mrs. Snell. "How come he did it? I mean what was he runnin' away about?"

Boo Boo blew a single, faulty smoke-ring at a pane of glass. "Some child in the park that afternoon had come up to him with the dreamy misinformation, 'You stink, kid.' At least, that's why we think he did it. I don't know, Mrs. Snell. It's all slightly over my head."

"How long's he been doin' it?" asked Mrs. Snell. "I mean how long's he been doin' it?"

"Well, at the age of two-and-a-half," Boo Boo said biographically, "he sought refuge under a sink in the basement of our apartment house. Down in the laun-dry. Naomi somebody—a close friend of his—told him she had a worm in her thermos bottle. At least, that's all we could get out of him." Boo Boo sighed, and came away from the window with a long ash on her cigarette. She started for the screen door. "I'll have another go at it," she said, by way of goodby to both women.

They laughed.

"Mildred," Sandra, still laughing, addressed Mrs. Snell, "you're gonna miss your bus if ya don't get a move on."

Boo Boo closed the screen door behind her.

She stood on the slight downgrade of her front lawn, with the low, glaring, late afternoon sun at her back. About two hundred yards ahead of her, her son Lionel was sitting in the stern seat of his father's dinghy. Tied, and stripped of its main and jib sails, the dinghy floated at a perfect right angle away from the far end of the pier. Fifty feet or so beyond it, a lost or aban-

doned water ski floated bottom up, but there were no
pleasure boats to be seen on the lake; just a stern-end
view of the county launch on its way over to Leech's
Landing. Boo Boo found it queerly difficult to keep
Lionel in steady focus. The sun, though not especially
hot, was nonetheless so brilliant that it made any fairly
distant image—a boy, a boat—seem almost as wav-
ering and refractional as a stick in water. After a
couple of minutes, Boo Boo let the image go. She
peeled down her cigarette Army style, and then started
toward the pier.

It was October, and the pier boards no longer could
hit her in the face with reflected heat. She walked
along whistling "Kentucky Babe" through her teeth.
When she reached the end of the pier, she squatted,
her knees audible, at the right edge, and looked down
at Lionel. He was less than an oar's length away from
her. He didn't look up.

"Ahoy," Boo Boo said. "Friend. Pirate. Dirty dog.
I'm back."

Still not looking up, Lionel abruptly seemed called
upon to demonstrate his sailing ability. He swung the
dead tiller all the way to the right, then immediately
yanked it back in to his side. He kept his eyes exclusively on the deck of the boat.

"It is I," Boo Boo said. "Vice-Admiral Tannenbaum.
Née Glass. Come to inspect the stermaphors."

There was a response.

"You aren't an admiral. You're a *lady*," Lionel said.
His sentences usually had at least one break of faulty
breath control, so that, often, his emphasized words,
instead of rising, sank. Boo Boo not only listened to
his voice, she seemed to watch it.

"Who told you that? Who told you I wasn't an
admiral?"

Lionel answered, but inaudibly.

"Who?" said Boo Boo.

"Daddy."

Still in a squatting position, Boo Boo put her left hand through the V of her legs, touching the pier boards in order to keep her balance. "Your daddy's a nice fella," she said, "but he's probably the biggest landlubber I know. It's perfectly true that when I'm in port I'm a lady—*that's* true. But my true calling is first, last, and always the bounding—"

"You aren't an admiral," Lionel said.

"I beg your pardon?"

"You aren't an admiral. You're a lady all the time."

There was a short silence. Lionel filled it by changing the course of his craft again—his hold on the tiller was a two-armed one. He was wearing khaki-colored shorts and a clean, white T-shirt with a dye picture, across the chest, of Jerome the Ostrich playing the violin. He was quite tanned, and his hair, which was almost exactly like his mother's in color and quality, was a little sun-bleached on top.

"Many people think I'm not an admiral," Boo Boo said, watching him. "Just because I don't shoot my mouth off about it." Keeping her balance, she took a cigarette and matches out of the side pocket of her jeans. "I'm almost never tempted to discuss my rank with people. Especially with little boys who don't even look at me when I talk to them. I'd be drummed out of the bloomin' service." Without lighting her cigarette, she suddenly got to her feet, stood unreasonably erect, made an oval out of the thumb and index finger of her right hand, drew the oval to her mouth, and—kazoo style—sounded something like a bugle call. Lionel instantly looked up. In all probability, he was

aware that the call was bogus, but nonetheless he seemed deeply aroused; his mouth fell open. Boo Boo sounded the call—a peculiar amalgamation of "Taps" and "Reveille"—three times, without any pauses. Then, ceremoniously, she saluted the opposite shoreline. When she finally reassumed her squat on the pier edge, she seemed to do so with maximum regret, as if she had just been profoundly moved by one of the virtues of naval tradition closed to the public and small boys. She gazed out at the petty horizon of the lake for a moment, then seemed to remember that she was not absolutely alone. She glanced—venerably—down at Lionel, whose mouth was still open. "That was a secret bugle call that only admirals are allowed to hear." She lit her cigarette, and blew out the match with a theatrically thin, long stream of smoke. "If anybody knew I let you hear that call—" She shook her head. She again fixed the sextant of her eye on the horizon.

"Do it again."

"Impossible."

"Why?"

Boo Boo shrugged. "Too many low-grade officers around, for one thing." She changed her position, taking up a cross-legged, Indian squat. She pulled up her socks. "I'll tell you what I'll do, though," she said, matter-of-factly. "If you'll tell me why you're running away, I'll blow every secret bugle call for you I know. All right?"

Lionel immediately looked down at the deck again. "No," he said.

"Why not?"

"Because."

"Because why?"

"Because I don't want to," said Lionel, and jerked the tiller for emphasis.

Boo Boo shielded the right side of her face from the glare of the sun. "You told me you were all through running away," she said. "We talked about it, and you told me you were all through. You promised me."

Lionel gave a reply, but it didn't carry.

"What?" said Boo Boo.

"I didn't promise."

"Ah, yes, you did. You most certainly did."

Lionel resumed steering his boat. "If you're an admiral," he said, "where's your *fleet?*"

"My fleet. I'm glad you asked me that," Boo Boo said, and started to lower herself into the dinghy.

"Get off!" Lionel ordered, but without giving over to shrillness, and keeping his eyes down. "Nobody can come in."

"They can't?" Boo Boo's foot was already touching the bow of the boat. She obediently drew it back up to pier level. "Nobody at all?" She got back into her Indian squat. "Why not?"

Lionel's answer was complete, but, again, not loud enough.

"What?" said Boo Boo.

"Because they're not allowed."

Boo Boo, keeping her eyes steadily on the boy, said nothing for a full minute.

"I'm sorry to hear it," she said, finally. "I'd just love to come down in your boat. I'm so lonesome for you. I miss you so much. I've been all alone in the house all day without anybody to talk to."

Lionel didn't swing the tiller. He examined the grain of wood in its handle. "You can talk to Sandra," he said.

"Sandra's busy," Boo Boo said. "Anyway, I don't want to talk to Sandra, I want to talk to you. I wanna come down in your boat and talk to you."

"You can talk from there."

"What?"

"You can talk from *there*."

"No, I can't. It's too big a distance. I have to get up close."

Lionel swung the tiller. "Nobody can come in," he said.

"What?"

"Nobody can come *in*."

"Well, will you tell me from there why you're running away?" Boo Boo asked. "After you promised me you were all through?"

A pair of underwater goggles lay on the deck of the dinghy, near the stern seat. For answer, Lionel secured the headstrap of the goggles between the big and second toes of his right foot, and, with a deft, brief, leg action, flipped the goggles overboard. They sank at once.

"That's nice. That's constructive," said Boo Boo. "Those belong to your Uncle Webb. Oh, he'll be so delighted." She dragged on her cigarette. "They once belonged to your Uncle Seymour."

"I don't care."

"I see that. I see you don't," Boo Boo said. Her cigarette was angled peculiarly between her fingers; it burned dangerously close to one of her knuckle grooves. Suddenly feeling the heat, she let the cigarette drop to the surface of the lake. Then she took out something from one of her side pockets. It was a package, about the size of a deck of cards, wrapped in white paper and tied with green ribbon. "This is a key chain," she said, feeling the boy's eyes look up at her. "Just like Daddy's. But with a lot more keys on it than Daddy's has. This one has ten keys."

Lionel leaned forward in his seat, letting go the tiller. He held out his hands in catching position. "Throw it?" he said. "Please?"

"Let's keep our seats a minute, Sunshine. I have a little thinking to do. I *should* throw this key chain in the lake."

Lionel stared up at her with his mouth open. He closed his mouth. "It's mine," he said on a diminishing note of justice.

Boo Boo, looking down at him, shrugged. "I don't care."

Lionel slowly sat back in his seat, watching his mother, and reached behind him for the tiller. His eyes reflected pure perception, as his mother had known they would.

"Here." Boo Boo tossed the package down to him. It landed squarely on his lap.

He looked at it in his lap, picked it off, looked at it in his hand, and flicked it—sidearm—into the lake. He then immediately looked up at Boo Boo, his eyes filled not with defiance but tears. In another instant, his mouth was distorted into a horizontal figure-8, and he was crying mightily.

Boo Boo got to her feet, gingerly, like someone whose foot has gone to sleep in theatre, and lowered herself into the dinghy. In a moment, she was in the stern seat, with the pilot on her lap, and she was rocking him and kissing the back of his neck and giving out certain information: "Sailors don't *cry*, baby. Sailors *never* cry. Only when their ships go down. Or when they're shipwrecked, on rafts and all, with nothing to drink except—"

"Sandra—told Mrs. Smell—that Daddy's a big— sloppy—kike."

Just perceptibly, Boo Boo flinched, but she lifted the boy off her lap and stood him in front of her and pushed back his hair from his forehead. "She did, huh?" she said.

Lionel worked his head up and down, emphatically. He came in closer, still crying, to stand between his mother's legs.

"Well, that isn't *too* terrible," Boo Boo said, holding him between the two vises of her arms and legs. "That isn't the *worst* that could happen." She gently bit the rim of the boy's ear. "Do you know what a kike is, baby?"

Lionel was either unwilling or unable to speak up at once. At any rate, he waited till the hiccupping aftermath of his tears had subsided a little. Then his answer was delivered, muffled but intelligible, into the warmth of Boo Boo's neck. "It's one of those things that go up in the *air*," he said. "With *string* you hold."

The better to look at him, Boo Boo pushed her son slightly away from her. Then she put a wild hand inside the seat of his trousers, startling the boy considerably, but almost immediately withdrew it and decorously tucked in his shirt for him. "Tell you what we'll do," she said. "We'll drive to town and get some pickles, and some bread, and we'll eat the pickles in the car, and then we'll go to the station and get Daddy, and then we'll bring Daddy home and make him take us for a ride in the boat. You'll have to help him carry the sails down. O.K.?"

"O.K.," said Lionel.

They didn't walk back to the house; they raced. Lionel won.

For Esmé—with Love and Squalor

JUST RECENTLY, by air mail, I received an invitation to a wedding that will take place in England on April 18th. It happens to be a wedding I'd give a lot to be able to get to, and when the invitation first arrived, I thought it might just be possible for me to make the trip abroad, by plane, expenses be hanged. However, I've since discussed the matter rather extensively with my wife, a breathtakingly levelheaded girl, and we've decided against it—for one thing, I'd completely forgotten that my mother-in-law is looking forward to spending the last two weeks in April with us. I really don't get to see Mother Grencher terribly often, and she's not getting any younger. She's fifty-eight. (As she'd be the first to admit.)

All the same, though, wherever I happen to be I don't think I'm the type that doesn't even lift a finger to prevent a wedding from flatting. Accordingly, I've gone ahead and jotted down a few revealing notes on the bride as I knew her almost six years ago. If my notes should cause the groom, whom I haven't met, an uneasy moment or two, so much the better. Nobody's aiming to please, here. More, really, to edify, to instruct.

In April of 1944, I was among some sixty American enlisted men who took a rather specialized pre-Invasion training course, directed by British Intelligence, in Devon, England. And as I look back, it seems to me that we were fairly unique, the sixty of us, in that there wasn't one good mixer in the bunch. We were all essentially letter-writing types, and when we spoke to each other out of the line of duty, it was usually to ask somebody if he had any ink he wasn't using. When we weren't writing letters or attending classes, each of us went pretty much his own way. Mine usually led me, on clear days, in scenic circles around the countryside. Rainy days, I generally sat in a dry place and read a book, often just an axe length away from a ping-pong table.

The training course lasted three weeks, ending on a Saturday, a very rainy one. At seven that last night, our whole group was scheduled to entrain for London, where, as rumor had it, we were to be assigned to infantry and airborne divisions mustered for the D Day landings. By three in the afternoon, I'd packed all my belongings into my barrack bag, including a canvas gas-mask container full of books I'd brought over from the Other Side. (The gas mask itself I'd slipped through a porthole of the *Mauretania* some weeks earlier, fully aware that if the enemy ever *did* use gas I'd never get the damn thing on in time.) I remember standing at an end window of our Quonset hut for a very long time, looking out at the slanting, dreary rain, my trigger finger itching imperceptibly, if at all. I could hear behind my back the uncomradely scratching of many fountain pens on many sheets of V-mail paper. Abruptly, with nothing special in mind, I came away from the window and put on my raincoat, cashmere muffler, galoshes, woollen gloves, and overseas cap (the last of which, I'm still told, I wore at an angle all my own—slightly down over both ears). Then, after synchronizing my wristwatch with the clock in the latrine, I walked down the long, wet cobblestone hill into town. I ignored the flashes of lightning all around me. They either had your number on them or they didn't.

In the center of town, which was probably the wettest part of town, I stopped in front of a church to read the bulletin board, mostly because the featured numerals, white on black, had caught my attention but partly because, after three years in the Army, I'd become addicted to reading bulletin boards. At three-fifteen, the board stated, there would be children's-choir practice. I looked at my wristwatch, then back at the board. A sheet of paper was tacked up, listing the names of the children expected to attend practice. I stood in the rain and read all the names, then entered the church.

A dozen or so adults were among the pews, several of them bearing pairs of small-size rubbers, soles up, in their laps. I passed along and sat down in the front row. On the rostrum, seated in three compact rows of auditorium chairs, were about twenty children, mostly girls, ranging in age from about seven to thirteen. At the moment, their choir coach, an enormous woman in tweeds, was advising them to open their mouths wider when they sang. Had anyone, she asked, ever heard of a little dickeybird that *dared* to sing his charming song without first opening his little beak wide, wide, wide? Apparently nobody ever had. She was given a steady, opaque look. She went on to say that she wanted *all* her children to absorb the *meaning* of the words they sang, not just *mouth* them, like silly-billy parrots. She then blew a note on her pitch pipe, and the children, like so many underage weight-lifters, raised their hymnbooks.

They sang without instrumental accompaniment—or, more accurately in their case, without any interference. Their voices were melodious and unsentimental, almost to the point where a somewhat more denominational man than myself might, without straining, have experienced levitation. A couple of the very youngest children dragged the tempo a trifle, but in a way that only the composer's mother could have found fault with. I had never heard the hymn, but I kept hoping it was one with a dozen or more verses. Listening, I scanned all the children's faces but watched one in particular, that of the child nearest me, on the end seat in the first row. She was about thirteen, with straight ash-blond hair of ear-lobe length, an exquisite forehead, and blasé eyes that, I thought, might very possibly have counted the house. Her voice was distinctly separate from the other children's voices, and not just because she was seated nearest me. It had the best upper register, the sweetest-sounding, the surest, and it automatically led the way. The young lady, however, seemed slightly bored with her own singing ability, or perhaps just with the time and place; twice, between verses, I saw her yawn. It was a ladylike yawn, a closed-mouth yawn, but you couldn't miss it; her nostril wings gave her away.

The instant the hymn ended, the choir coach began to give her lengthy opinion of people who can't keep their feet still and their lips sealed tight during the minister's sermon. I gathered that the singing part of the rehearsal was over, and before the coach's dissonant speaking voice could entirely break the spell the children's singing had cast, I got up and left the church.

It was raining even harder. I walked down the street and looked through the window of the Red Cross recreation room, but soldiers were standing two and three deep at the coffee counter, and, even through the glass, I could hear ping-pong balls bouncing in another room. I crossed the street and entered a civilian tearoom, which was empty except for a middle-aged waitress, who looked as if she would have preferred a customer with a dry raincoat. I used a coat tree as delicately as possible, and then sat down at a table and ordered tea and cinnamon toast. It was the first time all day that I'd spoken to anyone. I then looked through all my pockets, including my raincoat, and finally found a couple of stale letters to reread, one from my wife, telling me how the service at Schrafft's Eighty-eighth Street had fallen off, and one from my mother-in-law, asking me to please send her some cashmere yarn first chance I got away from "camp."

While I was still on my first cup of tea, the young lady I had been watching and listening to in the choir came into the tearoom. Her hair was soaking wet, and the rims of both ears were showing. She was with a very small boy, unmistakably her brother, whose cap she removed by lifting it off his head with two fingers, as if it were a laboratory specimen. Bringing up the rear was an efficient-looking woman in a limp felt hat —presumably their governess. The choir member, taking off her coat as she walked across the floor, made the table selection—a good one, from my point of view, as it was just eight or ten feet directly in front of me. She and the governess sat down. The small boy, who was about five, wasn't ready to sit down yet. He slid out of and discarded his reefer; then, with the dead-pan expression of a born heller, he methodically went about annoying his governess by pushing in and pull-ing out his chair several times, watching her face. The governess, keeping her voice down, gave him two or three orders to sit down and, in effect, stop the mon-key business, but it was only when his sister spoke to him that he came around and applied the small of his back to his chair seat. He immediately picked up his napkin and put it on his head. His sister removed it, opened it, and spread it out on his lap.

About the time their tea was brought, the choir member caught me staring over at her party. She stared back at me, with those house-counting eyes of hers, then, abruptly, gave me a small, qualified smile. It was oddly radiant, as certain small, qualified smiles sometimes are. I smiled back, much less radi-antly, keeping my upper lip down over a coal-black G.I. temporary filling showing between two of my front teeth. The next thing I knew, the young lady was standing, with enviable poise, beside my table. She was wearing a tartan dress—a Campbell tartan, I be-lieve. It seemed to me to be a wonderful dress for a very young girl to be wearing on a rainy, rainy day. "I thought Americans despised tea," she said.

It wasn't the observation of a smart aleck but that of a truth-lover or a statistics-lover. I replied that some of us never drank anything *but* tea. I asked her if she'd care to join me.

"Thank you," she said. "Perhaps for just a frac-tion of a moment."

I got up and drew a chair for her, the one opposite me, and she sat down on the forward quarter of it, keeping her spine easily and beautifully straight. I went back—almost hurried back—to my own chair, more than willing to hold up my end of a conversation. When I was seated, I couldn't think of anything to say, though. I smiled again, still keeping my coal-black filling under concealment. I remarked that it was certainly a terrible day out.

"Yes; quite," said my guest, in the clear, unmistakable voice of a small-talk detester. She placed her fingers flat on the table edge, like someone at a séance, then, almost instantly, closed her hands—her nails were bitten down to the quick. She was wearing a wristwatch, a military-looking one that looked rather like a navigator's chronograph. Its face was much too large for her slender wrist. "You were at choir practice," she said matter-of-factly. "I saw you."

I said I certainly had been, and that I had heard her voice singing separately from the others. I said I thought she had a very fine voice.

She nodded. "I know. I'm going to be a professional singer."

"Really? Opera?"

"Heavens, no. I'm going to sing jazz on the radio and make heaps of money. Then, when I'm thirty, I shall retire and live on a ranch in Ohio." She touched the top of her soaking-wet head with the flat of her hand. "Do you know Ohio?" she asked.

I said I'd been through it on the train a few times but that I didn't really know it. I offered her a piece of cinnamon toast.

"No, thank you," she said. "I eat like a bird, actually."

I bit into a piece of toast myself, and commented that there's some mighty rough country around Ohio.

"I know. An American I met told me. You're the eleventh American I've met."

Her governess was now urgently signalling her to return to her own table—in effect, to stop bothering the man. My guest, however, calmly moved her chair an inch or two so that her back broke all possible further communication with the home table. "You go to that secret Intelligence school on the hill, don't you?" she inquired coolly.

As security-minded as the next one, I replied that I was visiting Devonshire for my health.

"*Really*," she said, "I wasn't quite born yesterday, you know."

I said I'd bet she hadn't been, at that. I drank my tea for a moment. I was getting a trifle posture-conscious and I sat up somewhat straighter in my seat.

"You seem quite intelligent for an American," my guest mused.

I told her that was a pretty snobbish thing to say, if you thought about it at all, and that I hoped it was unworthy of her.

She blushed—automatically conferring on me the social poise I'd been missing. "Well. Most of the Americans *I've* seen act like animals. They're forever punching one another about, and insulting everyone, and—You know what one of them did?"

I shook my head.

"One of them threw an empty whiskey bottle through my aunt's window. *For*tunately, the window was open. But does that sound very intelligent to you?"

It didn't especially, but I didn't say so. I said that many soldiers, all over the world, were a long way from home, and that few of them had had many real advantages in life. I said I'd thought that most people could figure that out for themselves.

"Possibly," said my guest, without conviction. She raised her hand to her wet head again, picked at a few limp filaments of blond hair, trying to cover her exposed ear rims. "My hair is soaking wet," she said. "I look a fright." She looked over at me. "I have quite wavy hair when it's dry."

"I can see that, I can see you have."

"Not actually curly, but quite wavy," she said. "Are you married?"

I said I was.

She nodded. "Are you very deeply in love with your wife? Or am I being too personal?"

I said that when she was, I'd speak up.

She put her hands and wrists farther forward on the table, and I remember wanting to do something about that enormous-faced wristwatch she was wearing—perhaps suggest that she try wearing it around her waist.

"Usually, I'm not terribly gregarious," she said, and looked over at me to see if I knew the meaning of the word. I didn't give her a sign, though, one way or the other. "I purely came over because I thought you looked extremely lonely. You have an extremely sensitive face."

I said she was right, that I *had* been feeling lonely, and that I was very glad she'd come over.

"I'm training myself to be more compassionate. My aunt says I'm a terribly cold person," she said and felt the top of her head again. "I live with my aunt. She's an extremely kind person. Since the death of my mother, she's done everything within her power to make Charles and me feel adjusted."

"I'm glad."

"Mother was an extremely intelligent person. Quite sensuous, in many ways." She looked at me with a kind of fresh acuteness. "Do you find me terribly cold?"

I told her absolutely not—very much to the contrary, in fact. I told her my name and asked for hers.

She hesitated. "My first name is Esmé. I don't think I shall tell you my full name, for the moment. I have a title and you may just be impressed by titles. Americans are, you know."

I said I didn't think I would be, but that it might be a good idea, at that, to hold on to the title for a while.

Just then, I felt someone's warm breath on the back of my neck. I turned around and just missed brushing noses with Esmé's small brother. Ignoring me, he addressed his sister in a piercing treble: "Miss Megley said you must come and finish your tea!" His message delivered, he retired to the chair between his sister and me, on my right. I regarded him with high interest. He was looking very splendid in brown Shetland shorts, a navy-blue jersey, white shirt, and striped necktie. He gazed back at me with immense green eyes. "Why do people in films kiss sideways?" he demanded.

"Sideways?" I said. It was a problem that had baffled me in my childhood. I said I guessed it was because actors' noses are too big for kissing anyone head on.

"His name is Charles," Esmé said. "He's extremely brilliant for his age."

"He certainly has green eyes. Haven't you, Charles?"

Charles gave me the fishy look my question deserved, then wriggled downward and forward in his chair till all of his body was under the table except his head, which he left, wrestler's-bridge style, on the chair seat. "They're orange," he said in a strained voice, addressing the ceiling. He picked up a corner of the tablecloth and put it over his handsome, dead-pan little face.

"Sometimes he's brilliant and sometimes he's not," Esmé said. "Charles, do sit up!"

Charles stayed right where he was. He seemed to be holding his breath.

"He misses our father very much. He was s-l-a-i-n in North Africa."

I expressed regret to hear it.

Esmé nodded. "Father adored him." She bit reflectively at the cuticle of her thumb. "He looks very much like my mother—Charles, I mean. I look exactly like my father." She went on biting at her cuticle. "My mother was quite a passionate woman. She was an extrovert. Father was an introvert. They were quite well mated, though, in a superficial way. To be quite candid, Father really needed more of an intellectual companion than Mother was. He was an extremely gifted genius."

I waited, receptively, for further information, but none came. I looked down at Charles, who was now resting the side of his face on his chair seat. When he saw that I was looking at him, he closed his eyes, sleepily, angelically, then stuck out his tongue—an appendage of startling length—and gave out what in *my* country would have been a glorious tribute to a myopic baseball umpire. It fairly shook the tearoom.

"Stop that," Esmé said, clearly unshaken. "He saw an American do it in a fish-and-chips queue, and now he does it whenever he's bored. Just stop it, now, or I shall send you directly to Miss Megley."

Charles opened his enormous eyes, as sign that he'd

heard his sister's threat, but otherwise didn't look especially alerted. He closed his eyes again, and continued to rest the side of his face on the chair seat.

I mentioned that maybe he ought to save it—meaning the Bronx cheer—till he started using his title regularly. That is, if he had a title, too.

Esmé gave me a long, faintly clinical look. "You have a dry sense of humor, haven't you?" she said—wistfully. "Father said I have no sense of humor at all. He said I was unequipped to meet life because I have no sense of humor."

Watching her, I lit a cigarette and said I didn't think a sense of humor was any use in a real pinch.

"Father said it was."

This was a statement of faith, not a contradiction, and I quickly switched horses. I nodded and said her father had probably taken the long view, while I was taking the short (whatever *that* meant).

"Charles misses him exceedingly," Esmé said, after a moment. "He was an exceedingly lovable man. He was extremely handsome, too. Not that one's appearance matters greatly, but he was. He had terribly penetrating eyes, for a man who was intransically kind."

I nodded. I said I imagined her father had had quite an extraordinary vocabulary.

"Oh, yes; quite," said Esmé. "He was an archivist —amateur, of course."

At that point, I felt an importunate tap, almost a punch, on my upper arm, from Charles' direction. I turned to him. He was sitting in a fairly normal position in his chair now, except that he had one knee tucked under him. "What did one wall say to the other wall?" he asked shrilly. "It's a riddle!"

I rolled my eyes reflectively ceilingward and re-

peated the question aloud. Then I looked at Charles
with a stumped expression and said I gave up.

"Meet you at the corner!" came the punch line,
at top volume.

It went over biggest with Charles himself. It struck
him as unbearably funny. In fact, Esmé had to come
around and pound him on the back, as if treating him
for a coughing spell. "Now, stop that," she said. She
went back to her own seat. "He tells that same riddle
to everyone he meets and has a fit every single time.
Usually he drools when he laughs. Now, just stop,
please."

"It's one of the best riddles I've heard, though," I
said, watching Charles, who was very gradually coming out of it. In response to this compliment, he sank
considerably lower in his chair and again masked his
face up to the eyes with a corner of the tablecloth.
He then looked at me with his exposed eyes, which
were full of slowly subsiding mirth and the pride of
someone who knows a really good riddle or two.

"May I inquire how you were employed before en-
tering the Army?" Esmé asked me.

I said I hadn't been employed at all, that I'd only
been out of college a year but that I like to think of
myself as a professional short-story writer.

She nodded politely. "Published?" she asked.

It was a familiar but always touchy question, and
one that I didn't answer just one, two, three. I started
to explain how most editors in America were a
bunch—

"My father wrote beautifully," Esmé interrupted.
"I'm saving a number of his letters for posterity."

I said that sounded like a very good idea. I happened to be looking at her enormous-faced, chrono-

graphic-looking wristwatch again. I asked if it had belonged to her father.

She looked down at her wrist solemnly. "Yes, it did," she said. "He gave it to me just before Charles and I were evacuated." Self-consciously, she took her hands off the table, saying, "Purely as a momento, of course." She guided the conversation in a different direction. "I'd be extremely flattered if you'd write a story exclusively for me sometime. I'm an avid reader."

I told her I certainly would, if I could. I said that I wasn't terribly prolific.

"It doesn't have to be terribly prolific! Just so that it isn't childish and silly." She reflected. "I prefer stories about squalor."

"About what?" I said, leaning forward.

"Squalor. I'm extremely interested in squalor."

I was about to press her for more details, but I felt Charles pinching me, hard, on my arm. I turned to him, wincing slightly. He was standing right next to me. "What did one wall say to the other wall?" he asked, not unfamiliarly.

"You asked him that," Esmé said. "Now, stop it."

Ignoring his sister, and stepping up on one of my feet, Charles repeated the key question. I noticed that his necktie knot wasn't adjusted properly. I slid it up into place, then, looking him straight in the eye, suggested, "Meetcha at the corner?"

The instant I'd said it, I wished I hadn't. Charles' mouth fell open. I felt as if I'd struck it open. He stepped down off my foot and, with white-hot dignity, walked over to his own table, without looking back.

"He's furious," Esmé said. "He has a violent temper. My mother had a propensity to spoil him. My father was the only one who didn't spoil him."

I kept looking over at Charles, who had sat down and started to drink his tea, using both hands on the cup. I hoped he'd turn around, but he didn't.

Esmé stood up. *"Il faut que je parte aussi,"* she said, with a sigh. "Do you know French?"

I got up from my own chair, with mixed feelings of regret and confusion. Esmé and I shook hands; her hand, as I'd suspected, was a nervous hand, damp at the palm. I told her, in English, how very much I'd enjoyed her company.

She nodded. "I thought you might," she said. "I'm quite communicative for my age." She gave her hair another experimental touch. "I'm dreadfully sorry about my hair," she said. "I've probably been hideous to look at."

"Not at all! As a matter of fact, I think a lot of the wave is coming back already."

She quickly touched her hair again. "Do you think you'll be coming here again in the immediate future?" she asked. "We come here every Saturday, after choir practice."

I answered that I'd like nothing better but that, unfortunately, I was pretty sure I wouldn't be able to make it again.

"In other words, you can't discuss troop movements," said Esmé. She made no move to leave the vicinity of the table. In fact, she crossed one foot over the other and, looking down, aligned the toes of her shoes. It was a pretty little execution, for she was wearing white socks and her ankles and feet were lovely. She looked up at me abruptly. "Would you like me to write to you?" she asked, with a certain amount of color in her face. "I write extremely articulate letters for a person my—"

"I'd love it." I took out pencil and paper and wrote down my name, rank, serial number, and A.P.O. number.

"I shall write to you first," she said, accepting it, "so that you don't feel *comp*romised in any way." She put the address into a pocket of her dress. "Goodbye," she said, and walked back to her table.

I ordered another pot of tea and sat watching the two of them till they, and the harassed Miss Megley, got up to leave. Charles led the way out, limping tragically, like a man with one leg several inches shorter than the other. He didn't look over at me. Miss Megley went next, then Esmé, who waved to me. I waved back, half getting up from my chair. It was a strangely emotional moment for me.

Less than a minute later, Esmé came back into the tearoom, dragging Charles behind her by the sleeve of his reefer. "Charles would like to kiss you goodbye," she said.

I immediately put down my cup, and said that was very nice, but was she *sure?*

"Yes," she said, a trifle grimly. She let go Charles' sleeve and gave him a rather vigorous push in my direction. He came forward, his face livid, and gave me a loud, wet smacker just below the right ear. Following this ordeal, he started to make a beeline for the door and a less sentimental way of life, but I caught the half belt at the back of his reefer, held on to it, and asked him, "What did one wall say to the other wall?"

His face lit up. "Meet you at the corner!" he shrieked, and raced out of the room, possibly in hysterics.

Esmé was standing with crossed ankles again. "You're quite sure you won't forget to write that story for me?" she asked. "It doesn't have to be ex*clus*ively for me. It can—"

I said there was absolutely no chance that I'd forget. I told her that I'd never written a story *for* anybody, but that it seemed like exactly the right time to get down to it.

She nodded. "Make it extremely squalid and moving," she suggested. "Are you at all acquainted with squalor?"

I said not exactly but that I was getting better acquainted with it, in one form or another, all the time, and that I'd do my best to come up to her specifications. We shook hands.

"Isn't it a pity that we didn't meet under less extenuating circumstances?"

I said it was, I said it certainly was.

"Goodbye," Esmé said. "I hope you return from the war with all your faculties intact."

I thanked her, and said a few other words, and then watched her leave the tearoom. She left it slowly, reflectively, testing the ends of her hair for dryness.

This is the squalid, or moving, part of the story, and the scene changes. The people change, too. I'm still around, but from here on in, for reasons I'm not at liberty to disclose, I've disguised myself so cunningly that even the cleverest reader will fail to recognize me.

It was about ten-thirty at night in Gaufurt, Bavaria, several weeks after V-E Day. Staff Sergeant X was in his room on the second floor of the civilian home in which he and nine other American soldiers had been quartered, even before the armistice. He was seated on a folding wooden chair at a small, messy-looking writing table, with a paperback overseas

novel open before him, which he was having great
trouble reading. The trouble lay with him, not the novel.
Although the men who lived on the first floor usually
had first grab at the books sent each month by Special
Services, X usually seemed to be left with the book he
might have selected himself. But he was a young man
who had not come through the war with all his faculties intact, and for more than an hour he had been
triple-reading paragraphs, and now he was doing it to
the sentences. He suddenly closed the book, without
marking his place. With his hand, he shielded his eyes
for a moment against the harsh, watty glare from the
naked bulb over the table.

He took a cigarette from a pack on the table and lit
it with fingers that bumped gently and incessantly
against one another. He sat back a trifle in his chair and
smoked without any sense of taste. He had been chain-
smoking for weeks. His gums bled at the slightest
pressure of the tip of his tongue, and he seldom
stopped experimenting; it was a little game he played,
sometimes by the hour. He sat for a moment smoking
and experimenting. Then, abruptly, familiarly, and, as
usual, with no warning, he thought he felt his mind dis-
lodge itself and teeter, like insecure luggage on an overhead rack. He quickly did what he had been doing for
weeks to set things right: he pressed his hands hard
against his temples. He held on tight for a moment.
His hair needed cutting, and it was dirty. He had washed
it three or four times during his two weeks' stay at the
hospital in Frankfort on the Main, but it had got
dirty again on the long, dusty jeep ride back to
Gaufurt. Corporal Z, who had called for him at the
hospital, still drove a jeep combat-style, with the
windshield down on the hood, armistice or no armistice. There were thousands of new troops in Germany.

By driving with his windshield down, combat-style, Corporal Z hoped to show that he was not one of them, that not by a long shot was he some new son of a bitch in the E.T.O.

When he let go of his head, X began to stare at the surface of the writing table, which was a catchall for at least two dozen unopened letters and at least five or six unopened packages, all addressed to him. He reached behind the debris and picked out a book that stood against the wall. It was a book by Goebbels, entitled "Die Zeit Ohne Beispiel." It belonged to the thirty-eight-year-old, unmarried daughter of the family that, up to a few weeks earlier, had been living in the house. She had been a low official in the Nazi Party, but high enough, by Army Regulations standards, to fall into an automatic-arrest category. X himself had arrested her. Now, for the third time since he had returned from the hospital that day, he opened the woman's book and read the brief inscription on the flyleaf. Written in ink, in German, in a small, hopelessly sincere handwriting, were the words "Dear God, life is hell." Nothing led up to or away from it. Alone on the page, and in the sickly stillness of the room, the words appeared to have the stature of an uncontestable, even classic indictment. X stared at the page for several minutes, trying, against heavy odds, not to be taken in. Then, with far more zeal than he had done anything in weeks, he picked up a pencil stub and wrote down under the inscription, in English, "Fathers and teachers, I ponder 'What is hell?' I maintain that it is the suffering of being unable to love." He started to write Dostoevski's name under the inscription, but saw—with fright that ran through his whole body—that what he had written was almost entirely illegible. He shut the book.

He quickly picked up something else from the table, a letter from his older brother in Albany. It had been on his table even before he had checked into the hospital. He opened the envelope, loosely resolved to read the letter straight through, but read only the top half of the first page. He stopped after the words "Now that the g.d. war is over and you probably have a lot of time over there, how about sending the kids a couple of bayonets or swastikas . . ." After he'd torn it up, he looked down at the pieces as they lay in the wastebasket. He saw that he had overlooked an enclosed snapshot. He could make out somebody's feet standing on a lawn somewhere.

He put his arms on the table and rested his head on them. He ached from head to foot, all zones of pain seemingly interdependent. He was rather like a Christmas tree whose lights, wired in series, must all go out if even one bulb is defective.

The door banged open, without having been rapped on. X raised his head, turned it, and saw Corporal Z standing in the door. Corporal Z had been X's jeep partner and constant companion from D Day straight through five campaigns of the war. He lived on the first floor and he usually came up to see X when he had a few rumors or gripes to unload. He was a huge, photogenic young man of twenty-four. During the war, a national magazine had photographed him in Hürtgen Forest; he had posed, more than just obligingly, with a Thanksgiving turkey in each hand. "Ya writin' letters?" he asked X. "It's spooky in here, for Chrissake." He preferred always to enter a room that had the overhead light on.

X turned around in his chair and asked him to

come in, and to be careful not to step on the dog.

"The what?"

"Alvin. He's right under your feet, Clay. How 'bout turning on the goddam light?"

Clay found the overhead-light switch, flicked it on, then stepped across the puny, servant's-size room and sat down on the edge of the bed, facing his host. His brick-red hair, just combed, was dripping with the amount of water he required for satisfactory grooming. A comb with a fountain-pen clip protruded, familiarly, from the right-hand pocket of his olive-drab shirt. Over the left-hand pocket he was wearing the Combat Infantrymen's Badge (which, technically, he wasn't authorized to wear), the European Theatre ribbon, with five bronze battle stars in it (instead of a lone silver one, which was the equivalent of five bronze ones), and the pre-Pearl Harbor service ribbon. He sighed heavily and said, "Christ almighty." It meant nothing; it was Army. He took a pack of cigarettes from his shirt pocket, tapped one out, then put away the pack and rebuttoned the pocket flap. Smoking, he looked vacuously around the room. His look finally settled on the radio. "Hey," he said. "They got this terrific show comin' on the radio in a coupla minutes. Bob Hope, and everybody."

X, opening a fresh pack of cigarettes, said he had just turned the radio off.

Undarkened, Clay watched X trying to get a cigarette lit. "Jesus," he said, with spectator's enthusiasm, "you oughta see your goddam hands. Boy, have you got the shakes. Ya know that?"

X got his cigarette lit, nodded, and said Clay had a real eye for detail.

"No kidding, hey. I goddam near fainted when I

saw you at the hospital. You looked like a goddam
corpse. How much weight ya lose? How many
pounds? Ya know?"

"I don't know. How was your mail when I was gone?
You heard from Loretta?"

Loretta was Clay's girl. They intended to get married at their earliest convenience. She wrote to him
fairly regularly, from a paradise of triple exclamation
points and inaccurate observations. All through the
war, Clay had read all Loretta's letters aloud to X,
however intimate they were—in fact, the more intimate, the better. It was his custom, after each reading, to ask X to plot out or pad out the letter of reply,
or to insert a few impressive words in French or German.

"Yeah, I had a letter from her yesterday. Down in
my room. Show it to ya later," Clay said, listlessly. He
sat up straight on the edge of the bed, held his breath,
and issued a long, resonant belch. Looking just semi-
pleased with the achievement, he relaxed again. "Her
goddam brother's gettin' outa the Navy on account of
his hip," he said. "He's got this hip, the bastard." He
sat up again and tried for another belch, but with be-
low-par results. A jot of alertness came into his face.
"Hey. Before I forget. We gotta get up at five
tomorrow and drive to Hamburg or someplace. Pick
up Eisenhower jackets for the whole detachment."

X, regarding him hostilely, stated that he didn't
want an Eisenhower jacket.

Clay looked surprised, almost a trifle hurt. "Oh,
they're good! They look good. How come?"

"No reason. Why do we have to get up at five?
The war's over, for God's sake."

"I don't know—we gotta get back before lunch.
They got some new forms in we gotta fill out before

lunch. . . . I asked Bulling how come we couldn't fill
'em out tonight—he's *got* the goddam forms right on
his desk. He don't want to open the envelopes yet,
the son of a bitch."

The two sat quiet for a moment, hating Bulling.

Clay suddenly looked at X with new—higher—interest than before. "Hey," he said. "Did you know
the goddam side of your face is jumping all over the
place?"

X said he knew all about it, and covered his tic with
his hand.

Clay stared at him for a moment, then said, rather
vividly, as if he were the bearer of exceptionally good
news, "I wrote Loretta you had a nervous break-
down."

"Oh?"

"Yeah. She's interested as hell in all that stuff.
She's majoring in psychology." Clay stretched himself
out on the bed, shoes included. "You know what
she said? She says nobody gets a nervous break-
down just from the war and all. She says you probably were unstable like, your whole goddam life."

X bridged his hands over his eyes—the light over
the bed seemed to be blinding him—and said that
Loretta's insight into things was always a joy.

Clay glanced over at him. "Listen, ya bastard," he
said. "She knows a goddam sight more psychology
than *you* do."

"Do you think you can bring yourself to take your
stinking feet off my bed?" X asked.

Clay left his feet where they were for a few don't-
tell-me-where-to-put-my-feet seconds, then swung them
around to the floor and sat up. "I'm goin' downstairs
anyway. They got the radio on in Walker's room."
He didn't get up from the bed, though. "Hey. I was just

tellin' that new son of a bitch, Bernstein, downstairs. Remember that time I and you drove into Valognes, and we got shelled for about two goddam hours, and that goddam cat I shot that jumped up on the hood of the jeep when we were layin' in that hole? Remember?"

"Yes—don't start that business with that cat again, Clay, God damn it. I don't want to hear about it."

"No, all I mean is I wrote Loretta about it. She and the whole psychology class discussed it. In class and all. The goddam professor and everybody."

"That's fine. I don't want to hear about it, Clay."

"No, you know the reason I took a pot shot at it, Loretta says? She says I was temporarily insane. No kidding. From the shelling and all."

X threaded his fingers, once, through his dirty hair, then shielded his eyes against the light again. "You weren't insane. You were simply doing your duty. You killed that pussycat in as manly a way as anybody could've under the circumstances."

Clay looked at him suspiciously. "What the hell are you talkin' about?"

"That cat was a spy. You *had* to take a pot shot at it. It was a very clever German midget dressed up in a cheap fur coat. So there was absolutely nothing brutal, or cruel, or dirty, or even—"

"God damn it!" Clay said, his lips thinned. "Can't you ever be *sincere?*"

X suddenly felt sick, and he swung around in his chair and grabbed the wastebasket—just in time.

When he had straightened up and turned toward his guest again, he found him standing, embarrassed, halfway between the bed and the door. X started to apologize, but changed his mind and reached for his cigarettes.

"C'mon down and listen to Hope on the radio, hey," Clay said, keeping his distance but trying to be friendly over it. "It'll do ya good. I mean it."

"You go ahead, Clay. . . . I'll look at my stamp collection."

"Yeah? You got a stamp collection? I didn't know you—"

"I'm only kidding."

Clay took a couple of slow steps toward the door. "I may drive over to Ehstadt later," he said. "They got a dance. It'll probably last till around two. Wanna go?"

"No, thanks. . . . I may practice a few steps in the room."

"O.K. G'night! Take it easy, now, for Chrissake." The door slammed shut, then instantly opened again. "Hey. O.K. if I leave a letter to Loretta under your door? I got some German stuff in it. Willya fix it up for me?"

"Yes. Leave me alone now, God damn it."

"Sure," said Clay. "You know what my mother wrote me? She wrote me she's glad you and I were together and all the whole war. In the same jeep and all. She says my letters are a helluva lot more intelligent since we been goin' around together."

X looked up and over at him, and said, with great effort, "Thanks. Tell her thanks for me."

"I will. G'night!" The door slammed shut, this time for good.

X sat looking at the door for a long while, then turned his chair around toward the writing table and picked up his portable typewriter from the floor. He made space for it on the messy table surface, pushing aside the collapsed pile of unopened letters and pack-

ages. He thought if he wrote a letter to an old friend
of his in New York there might be some quick, however slight, therapy in it for him. But he couldn't insert his notepaper into the roller properly, his fingers
were shaking so violently now. He put his hands down
at his sides for a minute, then tried again, but finally
crumpled the notepaper in his hand.

He was aware that he ought to get the wastebasket
out of the room, but instead of doing anything about it,
he put his arms on the typewriter and rested his head
again, closing his eyes.

A few throbbing minutes later, when he opened his
eyes, he found himself squinting at a small, unopened
package wrapped in green paper. It had probably
slipped off the pile when he had made space for the
typewriter. He saw that it had been readdressed several times. He could make out, on just one side of the
package, at least three of his old A.P.O. numbers.

He opened the package without any interest, without even looking at the return address. He opened it
by burning the string with a lighted match. He was
more interested in watching a string burn all the
way down than in opening the package, but he
opened it, finally.

Inside the box, a note, written in ink, lay on top of
a small object wrapped in tissue paper. He picked
out the note and read it.

17, —— ROAD,
——, DEVON
JUNE 7, 1944

DEAR SERGEANT X,
    I hope you will forgive me for having taken 38
days to begin our correspondence but, I have been

[112]

extremely busy as my aunt has undergone streptococcus of the throat and nearly perished and I have been justifiably saddled with one responsibility after another. However I have thought of you frequently and of the extremely pleasant afternoon we spent in each other's company on April 30, 1944 between 3:45 and 4:15 P.M. in case it slipped your mind.

We are all tremendously excited and overawed about D Day and only hope that it will bring about the swift termination of the war and a method of existence that is ridiculous to say the least. Charles and I are both quite concerned about you; we hope you were not among those who made the first initial assault upon the Cotentin Peninsula. Were you? Please reply as speedily as possible. My warmest regards to your wife.

Sincerely yours,

ESMÉ

P.S. I am taking the liberty of enclosing my wristwatch which you may keep in your possession for the duration of the conflict. I did not observe whether you were wearing one during our brief association, but this one is extremely water-proof and shockproof as well as having many other virtues among which one can tell at what velocity one is walking if one wishes. I am quite certain that you will use it to greater advantage in these difficult days than I ever can and that you will accept it as a lucky talisman.

Charles, whom I am teaching to read and write and whom I am finding an extremely intelligent novice, wishes to add a few words. Please write as soon as you have the time and inclination.

    HELLO HELLO HELLO HELLO HELLO
    HELLO HELLO HELLO HELLO HELLO
    LOVE AND KISSES CHALES

It was a long time before X could set the note aside, let alone lift Esmé's father's wristwatch out of the box. When he did finally lift it out, he saw that its crystal had been broken in transit. He wondered if the watch was otherwise undamaged, but he hadn't the courage to wind it and find out. He just sat with it in his hand for another long period. Then, suddenly, almost ecstatically, he felt sleepy.

You take a really sleepy man, Esmé, and he *al*ways stands a chance of again becoming a man with all his fac—with all his f-a-c-u-l-t-i-e-s intact.

Pretty Mouth and Green My Eyes

WHEN the phone rang, the gray-haired man asked the girl, with quite some little deference, if she would rather for any reason he didn't answer it. The girl heard him as if from a distance, and turned her face toward him, one eye—on the side of the light—closed tight, her open eye very, however disingenuously, large, and so blue as to appear almost violet. The gray-haired man asked her to hurry up, and she raised up on her right forearm just quickly enough so that the movement didn't quite look perfunctory. She cleared her hair back from her forehead with her left hand and said, "God. I don't know. I mean what do you think?" The gray-haired man said he didn't see that it made a helluva lot of difference one way or the other, and slipped his left hand under the girl's supporting arm, above the elbow, working his fingers up, making room for them between the warm surfaces of her upper arm and chest wall. He reached for the phone with his right hand. To reach it without groping, he had to raise himself somewhat higher, which caused the back of his head to graze a corner of the lampshade. In that instant, the light was particularly, if rather vividly, flattering to his gray, mostly white, hair. Though in dis-arrangement at that moment, it had obviously been freshly cut—or, rather, freshly maintained. The neck-line and temples had been trimmed conventionally close, but the sides and top had been left rather more than just longish, and were, in fact, a trifle "distin-guished-looking." "Hello?" he said resonantly into the phone. The girl stayed propped up on her forearm and watched him. Her eyes, more just open than alert or speculative, reflected chiefly their own size and color.

A man's voice—stone dead, yet somehow rudely, almost obscenely quickened for the occasion—came through at the other end: "Lee? I wake you?"

The gray-haired man glanced briefly left, at the girl. "Who's that?" he asked. "Arthur?"

"Yeah—I wake you?"

"No, no. I'm in bed, reading. Anything wrong?"

"You sure I didn't wake you? Honest to God?"

"No, no—absolutely," the gray-haired man said. "As a matter of fact, I've been averaging about four lousy hours—"

"The reason I called, Lee, did you happen to notice when Joanie was leaving? Did you happen to notice if she left with the Ellenbogens, by any chance?"

The gray-haired man looked left again, but high this time, away from the girl, who was now watching him rather like a young, blue-eyed Irish policeman. "No, I didn't, Arthur," he said, his eyes on the far, dim end of the room, where the wall met the ceiling. "Didn't she leave with you?"

"No. Christ, no. You didn't see her leave at all, then?"

"Well, no, as a matter of fact, I didn't, Arthur," the gray-haired man said. "Actually, as a matter of fact, I didn't see a bloody thing all evening. The minute I got in the door, I got myself involved in one long Jesus of a session with that French poop, Viennese poop—whatever the hell he was. Every bloody one of these foreign guys keep an eye open for a little free legal advice. Why? What's up? Joanie lost?"

"Oh, Christ. Who knows? I don't know. You know her when she gets all tanked up and rarin' to go. *I* don't know. She *may* have just—"

"You call the Ellenbogens?" the gray-haired man asked.

"Yeah. They're not home yet. I don't know. Christ, I'm not even sure she *left* with them. I know one thing. I know one goddam thing. I'm through beating my brains out. I mean it. I really mean it this time. I'm through. Five years. Christ."

"All right, try to take it a little easy, now, Arthur," the gray-haired man said. "In the first place, if I know the Ellenbogens, they probably all hopped in a cab and went down to the Village for a couple of hours. All three of 'em'll probably barge—"

"I have a feeling she went to work on some bastard in the kitchen. I just have a feeling. She always starts necking some bastard in the kitchen when she gets tanked up. I'm through. I swear to God I mean it this time. Five goddam—"

"Where are you now, Arthur?" the gray-haired man asked. "Home?"

"Yeah. Home. Home sweet home. Christ."

"Well, just try to take it a little—What are ya—drunk, or what?"

"I don't know. How the hell do I know?"

"All right, now, listen. Relax. Just relax," the gray-haired man said. "You know the Ellenbogens, for Chrissake. What probably happened, they probably missed their last train. All three of 'em'll probably barge in on you any minute, full of witty, night-club—"

"They drove in."

"How do you know?"

"Their baby-sitter. We've had some scintillating goddam conversations. We're close as hell. We're like two goddam peas in a pod."

"All right. All right. So what? Will ya sit tight and relax, now?" said the gray-haired man. "All three of 'em'll probably waltz in on you any minute. Take my word. You know Leona. I don't know what the hell it is—They all get this god-awful Connecticut *gaiety* when they get in to New York. You know that."

"Yeah. I know. I know. I don't know, though."

"Certainly you do. Use your imagination. The two of 'em probably dragged Joanie bodily—"

"Listen. Nobody ever has to *drag* Joanie *any*where. Don't gimme any of that dragging stuff."

"Nobody's giving you any dragging stuff, Arthur," the gray-haired man said quietly.

"I know, I know! Excuse me. Christ, I'm losing my mind. Honest to God, you sure I didn't wake you?"

"I'd tell you if you had, Arthur," the gray-haired man said. Absently, he took his left hand out from between the girl's upper arm and chest wall. "Look, Arthur. You want my advice?" he said. He took the telephone cord between his fingers, just under the transmitter. "I mean this, now. You want some advice?"

"Yeah. I don't know. Christ, I'm keeping you up. Why don't I just go cut my—"

"Listen to me a minute," the gray-haired man said. "First—I mean this, now—get in bed and relax. Make yourself a nice, big nightcap, and get under the—"

"*Night*cap! Are you kidding? Christ, I've killed about a quart in the last two goddam hours. *Night-cap!* I'm so plastered now I can hardly—"

"All right. All right. Get in bed, then," the gray-haired man said. "And relax—ya hear me? Tell the truth. Is it going to do any good to sit around and stew?"

"Yeah, I know. I wouldn't even worry, for Chris-sake, but you can't trust her! I swear to God. I swear to God you can't. You can trust her about as far as you can throw a—I don't know *what.* Aaah, what's the use? I'm losing my goddam mind."

"All right. Forget it, now. Forget it, now. Will ya do me a favor and try to put the whole thing out of your mind?" the gray-haired man said. "For all you know, you're making—I honestly think you're making a mountain—"

"You know what I do? *You know what I do?* I'm ashameda tell ya, but you know what I very nearly goddam do every night? When I get home? You want to know?"

"Arthur, listen, this isn't—"

"*Wait* a second—I'll *tell* ya, God damn it. I practically have to keep myself from opening every goddam closet door in the apartment—I swear to God. Every night I come home, I half expect to find a bunch of bastards hiding all over the place. *E*levator boys. De-*live*ry boys. *Cops*—"

"All right. All right. Let's try to take it a little easy, Arthur," the gray-haired man said. He glanced abrupt-ly to his right, where a cigarette, lighted some time earlier in the evening, was balanced on an ashtray. It obviously had gone out, though, and he didn't pick it up. "In the first place," he said into the phone, "I've told you many, many times, Arthur, that's ex*actly* where you make your biggest mistake. You know what you do? Would you like me to tell you what you do? You go out of your way—I mean this, now—You actually go out of your way to torture yourself. As a matter of fact, you actually in*spire* Joanie—" He broke off. "You're bloody lucky she's a wonderful kid. I mean it. You give that kid absolutely no credit for having any good taste—or *brains,* for Chrissake, for that matter—"

"Brains! Are you kidding? She hasn't got any goddam brains! She's an animal!"

The gray-haired man, his nostrils dilating, appeared to take a fairly deep breath. "We're all animals," he said. "Basically, we're all animals."

"Like hell we are. I'm no goddam animal. I may be a stupid, fouled-up twentieth-century son of a bitch, but I'm no animal. Don't gimme that. I'm no animal."

"Look, Arthur. This isn't getting us—"

"Brains. Jesus, if you knew how funny that was. She thinks she's a goddam intellectual. That's the funny part, that's the hilarious part. She reads the theatrical page, and she watches television till she's practically blind—so she's an intellectual. You know who I'm married to? You want to know who I'm married to? I'm married to the *greatest living undeveloped, undiscovered act*ress, *nove*list, psycho*an*alyst, and all-around goddam unappreciated celebrity-genius in New York. You didn't know that, didja? Christ, it's so funny I could cut my throat. Madame Bovary at Columbia Extension School. Madame—"

"Who?" asked the gray-haired man, sounding annoyed.

"Madame Bovary takes a course in Television Appreciation. God, if you knew how—"

"All right, all right. You realize this isn't getting

us anyplace," the gray-haired man said. He turned and gave the girl a sign, with two fingers near his mouth, that he wanted a cigarette. "In the first place," he said, into the phone, "for a helluvan intelligent guy, you're about as tactless as it's humanly possible to be." He straightened his back so that the girl could reach behind him for the cigarettes. "I mean that. It shows up in your private life, it shows up in your—"

"Brains. Oh, God, that kills me! Christ almighty! Did you ever hear her describe anybody—some man, I mean? Sometime when you haven't anything to do, do me a favor and get her to describe some man for you. She describes every man she sees as 'terribly attractive.' It can be the oldest, crummiest, greasiest—"

"All right, Arthur," the gray-haired man said sharply. "This is getting us nowhere. But nowhere." He took a lighted cigarette from the girl. She had lit two. "Just incidentally," he said, exhaling smoke through his nostrils, "how'd you make out today?"

"What?"

"How'd you make out today?" the gray-haired man repeated. "How'd the case go?"

"Oh, Christ! I don't know. Lousy. About two minutes before I'm all set to start my summation, the attorney for the plaintiff, Lissberg, trots in this crazy chambermaid with a bunch of bedsheets as evidence —bedbug stains all over them. Christ!"

"So what happened? You lose?" asked the gray-haired man, taking another drag on his cigarette.

"You know who was on the bench? Mother Vittorio. What the hell that guy has against me, I'll never know. I can't even open my mouth and he jumps all over me. You can't reason with a guy like that. It's impossible."

The gray-haired man turned his head to see what

the girl was doing. She had picked up the ashtray and was putting it between them. "You lose, then, or what?" he said into the phone.

"What?"

"I said, Did you lose?"

"Yeah. I was gonna tell you about it. I didn't get a chance at the party, with all the ruckus. You think Junior'll hit the ceiling? Not that I give a good goddam, but what do you think? Think he will?"

With his left hand, the gray-haired man shaped the ash of his cigarette on the rim of the ashtray. "I don't think he'll necessarily hit the *ceiling,* Arthur," he said quietly. "Chances are very much in favor, though, that he's not going to be overjoyed about it. You know how long we've handled those three bloody hotels? Old man Shanley himself started the whole—"

"I know, I know. Junior's told me about it at least fifty times. It's one of the most beautiful stories I ever heard in my life. All right, so I lost the goddam case. In the first place, it wasn't my fault. First, this lunatic Vittorio baits me all through the trial. Then this moron chambermaid starts passing out sheets full of bedbug—"

"Nobody's saying it's your fault, Arthur," the gray-haired man said. "You asked me if I thought Junior would hit the ceiling. I simply gave you an honest—"

"I know—I know that. . . . I don't know. What the hell. I may go back in the Army anyway. I tell you about that?"

The gray-haired man turned his head again toward the girl, perhaps to show her how forbearing, even stoic, his countenance was. But the girl missed seeing it. She had just overturned the ashtray with her knee and was rapidly, with her fingers, brushing the spilled ashes into a little pick-up pile; her eyes looked up at him a second too late. "No, you didn't, Arthur," he said into the phone.

"Yeah. I may. I don't know yet. I'm not crazy about the idea, naturally, and I won't go if I can possibly avoid it. But I may have to. I don't know. At least, it's oblivion. If they gimme back my little helmet and my big, fat desk and my nice, big mosquito net it might not—"

"I'd like to beat some sense into that head of yours, boy, that's what *I'd* like to do," the gray-haired man said. "For a helluvan—For a supposedly intelligent guy, you talk like an absolute child. And I say that in all sincerity. You let a bunch of minor little things snowball to an extent that they get so bloody paramount in your mind that you're absolutely unfit for any—"

"I shoulda left her. You know that? I should've gone through with it last summer, when I really had the ball rolling—you know that? You know why I didn't? You want to know why I didn't?"

"Arthur. For Chris*sake*. This is getting us exactly nowhere."

"Wait a second. Lemme tellya why! You want to know why I didn't? I can tellya exactly why. Because I felt sorry for her. That's the whole simple truth. I felt sorry for her."

"Well, I don't know. I mean that's out of my jurisdiction," the gray-haired man said. "It seems to me, though, that the one thing you seem to forget is that Joanie's a grown woman. I don't know, but it seems to me—"

"Grown woman! You crazy? She's a grown *child,* for Chrissake! Listen, I'll be shaving—listen to this— I'll be shaving, and all of a sudden she'll call me from way the hell the other end of the apartment. I'll go see what's the matter—right in the middle of shaving, lather all over my goddam face. You know what she'll want? She'll want to ask me if I think she has a good mind. I swear to God. She's *pathetic*, I tellya. I watch her when she's asleep, and I know what I'm talkin' about. Believe me."

"Well, that's something you know better than—I mean that's out of my jurisdiction," the gray-haired man said. "The point is, God damn it, you don't do anything at all constructive to—"

"We're mis*mated*, that's all. That's the whole simple story. We're just mismated as hell. You know what she needs? She needs some big silent bastard to just walk over once in a while and knock her out cold —then go back and finish reading his paper. That's what she needs. I'm too goddam weak for her. I knew it when we got married—I swear to God I did. I mean you're a smart bastard, you've never been married, but every now and then, before anybody gets married, they get these *flash*es of what it's going to be like after they're married. I ignored 'em. I ignored all my goddam flashes. I'm weak. That's the whole thing in a nutshell."

"You're not weak. You just don't use your head," the gray-haired man said, accepting a freshly lighted cigarette from the girl.

"Certainly I'm weak! Certainly I'm weak! God damn it, I know whether I'm weak or not! If I weren't weak, you don't think I'd've let everything get all—Aah, what's the usea talking? Certainly I'm weak . . . God, I'm keeping you awake all night. Why don't you hang the hell up on me? I mean it. Hang up on me."

"I'm not going to hang up on you, Arthur. I'd like to help you, if it's humanly possible," the gray-haired man said. "Actually, you're your own worst—"

"She doesn't respect me. She doesn't even love me, for God's sake. *Basically*—in the last analysis—I don't love her any more, either. I don't know. I do and I don't. It varies. It fluctuates. Christ! Every time I get all set to put my foot down, we have dinner out, for some reason, and I meet her somewhere and she comes in with these goddam white *gloves* on or something. I don't know. Or I start thinking about the first time we drove up to New Haven for the Princeton game. We had a flat right after we got off the Parkway, and it was cold as hell, and she held the flashlight while I fixed the goddam thing—You know what I mean. I don't know. Or I start thinking about—Christ, it's embarrassing—I start thinking about this goddam poem I sent her when we first started goin' around together. 'Rose my color is and white, Pretty mouth and green my eyes.' Christ, it's em*bar*rassing—it used to *remind* me of her. She doesn't have green eyes—she has eyes like goddam *sea* shells, for Chrissake—but it reminded me anyway . . . I don't know. What's the usea talking? I'm losing my mind. Hang up on me, why don't you? I mean it."

The gray-haired man cleared his throat and said, "I have no intention of hanging up on you, Arthur. There's just one—"

"She bought me a suit once. With her own money. I tell you about that?"

"No, I—"

"She just went into I think Tripler's and bought it. I didn't even go with her. I mean she has some goddam nice traits. The funny thing was it wasn't a bad fit. I just had to have it taken in a little bit around the seat—the pants—and the length. I mean she has some goddam nice traits."

The gray-haired man listened another moment.

Then, abruptly, he turned toward the girl. The look he gave her, though only glancing, fully informed her what was suddenly going on at the other end of the phone. "Now, Arthur. Listen. That isn't going to do any good," he said into the phone. "That isn't going to do any good. I mean it. Now, listen. I say this in all sincerity. Willya get undressed and get in bed, like a good guy? And relax? Joanie'll probably *be* there in about *two minutes*. You don't want her to see you like that, do ya? The bloody Ellenbogens'll probably barge in with her. You don't want the whole bunch of 'em to see you like that, do ya?" He listened. "Arthur? You hear me?"

"God, I'm keeping you awake all night. Everything I do, I—"

"You're *not* keeping me awake all night," the gray-haired man said. "Don't even think of that. I've already told you, I've been averaging about four hours' sleep a night. What I *would* like to do, though, if it's at all humanly possible, I'd like to help you, boy." He listened. "Arthur? You there?"

"Yeah. I'm here. Listen. I've kept you awake all night anyway. Could I come over to your place for a drink? Wouldja mind?"

The gray-haired man straightened his back and placed the flat of his free hand on the top of his head, and said, "Now, do you mean?"

"Yeah. I mean if it's all right with you. I'll only stay a minute. I'd just like to sit down somewhere and—I don't know. Would it be all right?"

"Yeah, but the point is I don't think you should, Arthur," the gray-haired man said, lowering his hand from his head. "I mean you're more than welcome to come, but I honestly think you should just sit tight and relax till Joanie waltzes in. I honestly do. What *you* want to be, you want to be right there on the spot when she waltzes in. Am I right, or not?"

"Yeah. I don't know. I swear to God, I don't know."

"Well, I do, I honestly do," the gray-haired man said. "Look. Why don't you hop in bed now, and relax, and then later, if you feel like it, give me a ring. I mean if you feel like talking. And *don't worry*. That's the main thing. Hear me? Willya do that now?"

"All right."

The gray-haired man continued for a moment to hold the phone to his ear, then lowered it into its cradle.

"What did he say?" the girl immediately asked him.

He picked his cigarette out of the ashtray—that is, selected it from an accumulation of smoked and half-smoked cigarettes. He dragged on it and said, "He wanted to come over here for a drink."

"God! What'd you say?" said the girl.

"You heard me," the gray-haired man said, and looked at her. "You could hear me. Couldn't you?" He squashed out his cigarette.

"You were wonderful. Absolutely marvellous," the girl said, watching him. "God, I feel like a dog!"

"Well," the gray-haired man said, "it's a tough situation. I don't know how marvellous I was."

"You were. You were wonderful," the girl said. "I'm *limp*. I'm absolutely *limp*. Look at me!"

The gray-haired man looked at her. "Well, actually, it's an impossible situation," he said. "I mean the whole thing's so fantastic it isn't even—"

"Darling—Excuse me," the girl said quickly, and leaned forward. "I think you're on *fire*." She gave the back of his hand a short, brisk, brushing stroke with the flats of her fingers. "No. It was just an ash." She leaned back. "No, you were marvellous," she said. "God, I feel like an absolute *dog!*"

"Well, it's a very, very tough situation. The guy's obviously going through absolute—"

The phone suddenly rang.

The gray-haired man said "Christ!" but picked it up before the second ring. "Hello?" he said into it.

"Lee? Were you asleep?"

"No, no."

"Listen, I just thought you'd want to know. Joanie just barged in."

"What?" said the gray-haired man, and bridged his left hand over his eyes, though the light was behind him.

"Yeah. She just barged in. About ten seconds after I spoke to you. I just thought I'd give you a ring while she's in the john. Listen, thanks a million, Lee. I mean it—you know what I mean. You weren't asleep, were ya?"

"No, no. I was just—No, no," the gray-haired man said, leaving his fingers bridged over his eyes. He cleared his throat.

"Yeah. What happened was, apparently Leona got stinking and then had a goddam crying jag, and Bob wanted Joanie to go out and grab a drink with them somewhere and iron the thing out. *I* don't know. *You* know. Very involved. Anyway, so she's home. What a rat race. Honest to God, I think it's this goddam New York. What I think maybe we'll do, if everything goes along all right, we'll get ourselves a little place in Connecticut maybe. Not too far out, necessarily, but far enough that we can lead a normal goddam life. I mean she's crazy about plants and all that stuff. She'd probably go mad if she had her own goddam garden

and stuff. Know what I mean? I mean—except you—
who do we know in New York except a bunch of
neurotics? It's bound to undermine even a normal person sooner or later. Know what I mean?"

The gray-haired man didn't give an answer. His
eyes, behind the bridge of his hand, were closed.

"Anyway, I'm gonna talk to her about it tonight.
Or tomorrow, maybe. She's still a little under the
weather. I mean she's a helluva good kid basically,
and if we *have* a chance to straighten ourselves out a
little bit, we'd be goddam stupid not to at least have a
go at it. While I'm at it, I'm also gonna try to
straighten out this lousy bedbug mess, too. I've been
thinking. I was just wondering, Lee. You think if I
went in and talked to Junior personally, I could—"

"Arthur, if you don't mind, I'd appreciate—"

"I mean I don't want you to think I just called you
back or anything because I'm *worried* about my goddam job or anything. I'm not. I mean basically, for
Chrissake, I couldn't care less. I just thought if I
could straighten Junior out without beating my brains
out, I'd be a goddam fool—"

"Listen, Arthur," the gray-haired man interrupted,
taking his hand away from his face, "I have a helluva
headache all of a sudden. I don't know where I got
the bloody thing from. You mind if we cut this short?
I'll talk to you in the morning—all right?" He listened
for another moment, then hung up.

Again the girl immediately spoke to him, but he
didn't answer her. He picked a burning cigarette—
the girl's—out of the ashtray and started to bring it to
his mouth, but it slipped out of his fingers. The girl
tried to help him retrieve it before anything was
burned, but he told her to just *sit still,* for Chrissake,
and she pulled back her hand.

De Daumier-Smith's
Blue Period

IF IT MADE any real sense—and it doesn't even begin
to—I think I might be inclined to dedicate this account, for whatever it's worth, especially if it's the
least bit ribald in parts, to the memory of my late,
ribald stepfather, Robert Agadganian, Jr. Bobby—as
everyone, even I, called him—died in 1947, surely
with a few regrets, but without a single gripe, of
thrombosis. He was an adventurous, extremely mag-
netic, and generous man. (After having spent so many
years laboriously begrudging him those picaresque adjectives, I feel it's a matter of life and death to get
them in here.)

My mother and father were divorced during the win-
ter of 1928, when I was eight, and mother married
Bobby Agadganian late that spring. A year later, in
the Wall Street Crash, Bobby lost everything he and
mother had, with the exception, apparently, of a magic
wand. In any case, practically overnight, Bobby turned
himself from a dead stockbroker and incapacitated

bon vivant into a live, if somewhat unqualified, agent-appraiser for a society of independent American art galleries and fine arts museums. A few weeks later, early in 1930, our rather mixed threesome moved from New York to Paris, the better for Bobby to ply his new trade. Being a cool, not to say an ice-cold, ten at the time, I took the big move, so far as I know, un-traumatically. It was the move back to New York, nine years later, three months after my mother died, that threw me, and threw me terribly.

I remember a significant incident that occurred just a day or two after Bobby and I arrived in New York. I was standing up in a very crowded Lexington Avenue bus, holding on to the enamel pole near the driver's seat, buttocks to buttocks with the chap behind me. For a number of blocks the driver had repeatedly given those of us bunched up near the front door a curt order to "step to the rear of the vehicle." Some of us had tried to oblige him. Some of us hadn't. At length, with a red light in his favor, the harassed man swung around in his seat and looked up at me, just behind him. At nineteen, I was a hatless type, with a flat, black, not particularly clean, Continental-type pompadour over a badly broken-out inch of fore-head. He addressed me in a lowered, an almost pru-dent tone of voice. "All right, buddy," he said, "let's move that ass." It was the "buddy," I think, that did it. Without even bothering to bend over a little—that is, to keep the conversation at least as private, as *de bon goût,* as *he'd* kept it—I informed him, in French, that he was a rude, stupid, overbearing imbecile, and that he'd never know how much I detested him. Then, rather elated, I stepped to the rear of the vehicle.

Things got much worse. One afternoon, a week or so later, as I was coming out of the Ritz Hotel, where

Bobby and I were indefinitely stopping, it seemed to me that all the seats from all the buses in New York had been unscrewed and taken out and set up in the street, where a monstrous game of Musical Chairs was in full swing. I think I might have been willing to join the game if I had been granted a special dispensation from the Church of Manhattan guaranteeing that all the other players would remain respectfully standing till I was seated. When it became clear that nothing of the kind was forthcoming, I took more direct action. I prayed for the city to be cleared of people, for the gift of being alone—a-l-o-n-e: which is the one New York prayer that rarely gets lost or delayed in channels, and in no time at all everything I touched turned to solid loneliness. Mornings and early afternoons, I attended—bodily—an art school on Forty-eighth and Lexington Avenue, which I loathed. (The week before Bobby and I had left Paris, I had won three first-prize awards at the National Junior Exhibition, held at the Freiburg Galleries. Throughout the voyage to America, I used our stateroom mirror to note my uncanny physical resemblance to El Greco.) Three late afternoons a week I spent in a dentist's chair, where, within a period of a few months, I had eight teeth extracted, three of them front ones. The other two afternoons I usually spent wandering through art galleries, mostly on Fifty-seventh Street, where I did all but hiss at the American entries. Evenings, I generally read. I bought a complete set of the *Harvard Classics*—chiefly because Bobby said we didn't have room for them in our suite—and rather perversely read all fifty volumes. Nights, I almost invariably set up my easel between the twin beds in the room I shared with Bobby, and painted. In one month alone, according to my diary for 1939, I completed eighteen

oil paintings. Noteworthily enough, seventeen of them
were self-portraits. Sometimes, however, possibly when
my Muse was being capricious, I set aside my paints
and drew cartoons. One of them I still have. It shows a
cavernous view of the mouth of a man being attended
by his dentist. The man's tongue is a simple, U.S.
Treasury hundred dollar bill, and the dentist is saying,
sadly, in French, "I think we can save the molar, but
I'm afraid that tongue will have to come out." It was
an enormous favorite of mine.

As roommates, Bobby and I were neither more nor
less compatible than would be, say, an exceptionally
live-and-let-live Harvard senior, and an exceptionally
unpleasant Cambridge newsboy. And when, as the
weeks went by, we gradually discovered that we were
both in love with the same deceased woman, it was no
help at all. In fact, a ghastly little after-*you*-Alphonse
relationship grew out of the discovery. We began to
exchange vivacious smiles when we bumped into each
other on the threshold of the bathroom.

One week in May of 1939, about ten months after
Bobby and I checked into the Ritz, I saw in a Quebec
newspaper (one of sixteen French-language news-
papers and periodicals I had blown myself a subscrip-
tion to) a quarter-column advertisement that had been
placed by the direction of a Montreal correspondence
art school. It advised all qualified instructors—it as
much as said, in fact, that it couldn't advise them
fortement enough—to apply immediately for employ-
ment at the newest, most progressive, correspondence
art school in Canada. Candidate instructors, it stipu-
lated, were to have a fluent knowledge of both the
French and English languages, and only those of tem-
perate habits and unquestionable character need

apply. The summer session at Les Amis Des Vieux Maîtres was officially to open on 10 June. Samples of work, it said, should represent both the academic and commercial fields of art, and were to be submitted to Monsieur I. Yoshoto, *directeur,* formerly of the Imperial Academy of Fine Arts, Tokyo.

Instantly, feeling almost insupportably qualified, I got out Bobby's Hermes-Baby typewriter from under his bed and wrote, in French, a long, intemperate letter to M. Yoshoto—cutting all my morning classes at the art school on Lexington Avenue to do it. My opening paragraph ran some three pages, and very nearly smoked. I said I was twenty-nine and a great-nephew of Honoré Daumier. I said I had just left my small estate in the South of France, following the death of my wife, to come to America to stay—temporarily, I made it clear—with an invalid relative. I had been painting, I said, since early childhood, but that, following the advice of Pablo Picasso, who was one of the oldest and dearest friends of my parents, I had never exhibited. However, a number of my oil paintings and water colors were now hanging in some of the finest, and by no means *nouveau riche,* homes in Paris, where they had *gagné* considerable attention from some of the most formidable critics of our day. Following, I said, my wife's untimely and tragic death, of an *ulcération cancéreuse,* I had earnestly thought I would never again set brush to canvas. But recent financial losses had led me to alter my earnest *résolution.* I said I would be most honored to submit samples of my work to Les Amis Des Vieux Maîtres, just as soon as they were sent to me by my agent in Paris, to whom I would write, of course, *très pressé.* I remained, most respectfully, *Jean de Daumier-Smith.*

It took me almost as long to select a pseudonym as it had taken me to write the whole letter.

I wrote the letter on overlay tissue paper. However, I sealed it in a Ritz envelope. Then, after applying a special-delivery stamp I'd found in Bobby's top drawer, I took the letter down to the main mail drop in the lobby. I stopped on the way to put the mail clerk (who unmistakably loathed me) on the alert for de Daumier-Smith's future incoming mail. Then, around two-thirty, I slipped into my one-forty-five anatomy class at the art school on Forty-eighth Street. My classmates seemed, for the first time, like a fairly decent bunch.

During the next four days, using all my spare time, plus some time that didn't quite belong to me, I drew a dozen or more samples of what I thought were typical examples of American commercial art. Working mostly in washes, but occasionally, to show off, in line, I drew people in evening clothes stepping out of limousines on opening nights—lean, erect, super-chic couples who had obviously never in their lives inflicted suffering as a result of underarm carelessness—couples, in fact, who perhaps didn't have any underarms. I drew suntanned young giants in white dinner jackets, seated at white tables alongside turquoise swimming pools, toasting each other, rather excitedly, with highballs made from a cheap but ostensibly ultra-fashionable brand of rye whisky. I drew ruddy, bill-board-genic children, beside themselves with delight and good health, holding up their empty bowls of breakfast food and pleading, good-naturedly, for more. I drew laughing, high-breasted girls aquaplaning without a care in the world, as a result of being amply protected against such national evils as bleeding gums, facial blemishes, unsightly hairs, and faulty or inadequate life insurance. I drew housewives who, until they reached for the right soap flakes, laid themselves wide open to straggly hair, poor posture, unruly children, disaffected husbands, rough (but slender) hands, untidy (but enormous) kitchens.

When the samples were finished, I mailed them immediately to M. Yoshoto, along with a half-dozen or so non-commercial paintings of mine that I'd brought with me from France. I also enclosed what I thought was a very casual note that only just began to tell the richly human little story of how, quite alone and variously handicapped, in the purest romantic tradition, I had reached the cold, white, isolating summits of my profession.

The next few days were horribly suspenseful, but before the week was out, a letter came from M. Yoshoto accepting me as an instructor at Les Amis Des Vieux Maîtres. The letter was written in English, even though I had written in French. (I later gathered that M. Yoshoto, who knew French but not English, had, for some reason, assigned the writing of the letter to Mme. Yoshoto, who had some working knowledge of English.) M. Yoshoto said that the summer session would probably be the busiest session of the year, and that it started on 24 June. This gave me almost five weeks, he pointed out, to settle my affairs. He offered me his unlimited sympathy for, in effect, my recent emotional and financial setbacks. He hoped that I would arrange myself to report at Les Amis Des Vieux Maîtres on Sunday, 23 June, in order to learn of my duties and to become "firm friends" with the other instructors (who, I later learned, were two in number, and consisted of M. Yoshoto and Mme. Yoshoto). He deeply regretted that it was not the school's policy to advance transportation fare to new instructors. Starting salary was twenty-eight dollars a week—which was not, M. Yoshoto said he realized, a very large sum of funds, but since it included bed and nourishing food, and since he sensed in me the true vocationary spirit, he hoped I would not feel cast down with vigor. He awaited a telegram of formal acceptance from me with eagerness and my arrival with a spirit of pleasantness, and remained, sincerely, my new friend and employer, I. Yoshoto, formerly of the Imperial Academy of Fine Arts, Tokyo.

My telegram of formal acceptance went out within five minutes. Oddly enough, in my excitement, or quite possibly from a feeling of guilt because I was using Bobby's phone to send the wire, I deliberately sat on my prose and kept the message down to ten words.

That evening when, as usual, I met Bobby for dinner at seven o'clock in the Oval Room, I was annoyed to see that he'd brought a guest along. I hadn't said or implied a word to him about my recent, extra-curricular doings, and I was dying to make this final news-break—to scoop him thoroughly—when we were alone. The guest was a very attractive young lady, then only a few months divorced, whom Bobby had been seeing a lot of and whom I'd met on several occasions. She was an altogether charming person whose every attempt to be friendly to me, to gently persuade me to take off my armor, or at least my helmet, I chose to interpret as an implied invitation to join her in bed at my earliest convenience—that is, as soon as Bobby, who clearly was too old for her, could be given the slip. I was hostile and laconic throughout dinner. At length, while we were having coffee, I tersely out-

lined my new plans for the summer. When I'd finished, Bobby put a couple of quite intelligent questions to me. I answered them coolly, overly briefly,
the unimpeachable crown prince of the situation.

"Oh, it sounds *very* exciting!" said Bobby's guest,
and waited, wantonly, for me to slip her my Montreal
address under the table.

"I thought you were going to Rhode Island with me,"
Bobby said.

"Oh, darling, don't be a horrible wet blanket," Mrs.
X said to him.

"I'm not, but I wouldn't mind knowing a little more
about it," Bobby said. But I thought I could tell from
his manner that he was already mentally exchanging
his train reservations for Rhode Island from a com-
partment to a lower berth.

"I think it's the sweetest, most *complimentary* thing
I ever heard in my life," Mrs. X said warmly to me.
Her eyes sparkled with depravity.

The Sunday that I stepped on to the platform at
Windsor Station in Montreal, I was wearing a double-
breasted, beige gabardine suit (that I had a damned
high opinion of), a navy-blue flannel shirt, a solid yellow, cotton tie, brown-and-white shoes, a Panama hat
(that belonged to Bobby and was rather too small for
me), and a reddish-brown moustache, aged three
weeks. M. Yoshoto was there to meet me. He was a
tiny man, not more than five feet tall, wearing a rather
soiled linen suit, black shoes, and a black felt hat with
the brim turned up all around. He neither smiled, nor,
as I remember, *said* anything to me as we shook
hands. His expression—and my word for it came
straight out of a French edition of Sax Rohmer's Fu
Manchu books—was *inscrutable*. For some reason, I

was smiling from ear to ear. I couldn't even turn it down, let alone off.

It was a bus ride of several miles from Windsor Station to the school. I doubt if M. Yoshoto said five words the whole way. Either in spite, or because, of his silence, I talked incessantly, with my legs crossed, ankle on knee, and constantly using my sock as an absorber for the perspiration on my palm. It seemed urgent to me not only to reiterate my earlier lies—about my kinship with Daumier, about my deceased wife, about my small estate in the South of France—but to elaborate on them. At length, in effect to spare myself from dwelling on these painful reminiscences (and they *were* beginning to feel a little painful), I swung over to the subject of my parents' oldest and dearest friend: Pablo Picasso. *Le pauvre Picasso,* as I referred to him. (I picked Picasso, I might mention, because he seemed to me the French painter who was best-known in America. I roundly considered Canada part of America.) For M. Yoshoto's benefit, I recalled, with a showy amount of natural compassion for a fallen giant, how many times I had said to him, *"M. Picasso, où allez vous?"* and how, in response to this all-penetrating question, the master had never failed to walk slowly, leadenly, across his studio to look at a small reproduction of his "Les Saltimbanques" and the glory, long forfeited, that had been his. The trouble with Picasso, I explained to M. Yoshoto as we got out of the bus, was that he never listened to anybody— even his closest friends.

In 1939, Les Amis Des Vieux Maîtres occupied the second floor of a small, highly unendowed-looking, three-story building—a tenement building, really—in the Verdun, or least attractive, section of Montreal. The school was directly over an orthopedic appliances shop. One large room and a tiny, boltless latrine were all there was to Les Amis Des Vieux Maîtres itself. Nonetheless, the moment I was inside, the place seemed wondrously presentable to me. There was a very good reason. The walls of the "instructors' room" were hung with many framed pictures—all water colors—done by M. Yoshoto. Occasionally, I still dream of a certain white goose flying through an extremely pale-blue sky, with—and it was one of the most daring and accomplished feats of craftsmanship I've ever seen—the blueness of the sky, or an ethos of the blueness of the sky, reflected in the bird's feathers. The picture was hung just behind Mme. Yoshoto's desk. It made the room—it and one or two other pictures close to it in quality.

Mme. Yoshoto, in a beautiful, black and cerise silk kimono, was sweeping the floor with a short-handled broom when M. Yoshoto and I entered the instructors' room. She was a gray-haired woman, surely a head taller than her husband, with features that looked rather more Malayan than Japanese. She left off sweeping and came forward, and M. Yoshoto briefly introduced us. She seemed to me every bit as *inscrutable* as M. Yoshoto, if not more so. M. Yoshoto then offered to show me to my room, which, he explained (in French) had recently been vacated by his son, who had gone to British Columbia to work on a farm. (After his long silence in the bus, I was grateful to hear him speak with any continuity, and I listened rather vivaciously.) He started to apologize for the fact that there were no chairs in his son's room— only floor cushions—but I quickly gave him to believe that for me this was little short of a godsend. (In fact, I think I said I hated chairs. I was so nervous that if he had informed me that his son's room was flooded, night and day, with a foot of water, I probably would have let out a little cry of pleasure. I probably would have said I had a rare foot disease, one that required my keeping my feet wet eight hours daily.) Then he led me up a creaky wooden staircase to my room. I told him on the way, pointedly enough, that I was a student of Buddhism. I later found out that both he and Mme. Yoshoto were Presbyterians.

Late that night, as I lay awake in bed, with Mme. Yoshoto's Japanese-Malayan dinner still *en masse* and riding my sternum like an elevator, one or the other of the Yoshotos began to moan in his or her sleep, just the other side of my wall. It was a high, thin, broken moan, and it seemed to come less from an adult than from either a tragic, subnormal infant or a small malformed animal. (It became a regular nightly performance. I never did find out which of the Yoshotos it came from, let alone why.) When it became quite unendurable to listen to from a supine position, I got out of bed, put on my slippers, and went over in the dark and sat down on one of the floor cushions. I sat crosslegged for a couple of hours and smoked cigarettes, squashing them out on the instep of my slipper and putting the stubs in the breast pocket of my pyjamas. (The Yoshotos didn't smoke, and there were no ashtrays anywhere on the premises.) I got to sleep around five in the morning.

At six-thirty, M. Yoshoto knocked on my door and advised me that breakfast would be served at six-forty-five. He asked me, through the door, if I'd slept well, and I answered, *"Oui!"* I then dressed—putting on my blue suit, which I thought appropriate for an instructor on the opening day of school, and a red Sulka tie my mother had given me—and, without washing, hurried down the hall to the Yoshotos' kitchen.

Mme. Yoshoto was at the stove, preparing a fish breakfast. M. Yoshoto, in his B.V.D.'s and trousers, was seated at the kitchen table, reading a Japanese newspaper. He nodded to me, non-committally. Neither of them had ever looked more *inscrutable*. Presently, some sort of fish was served to me on a plate with a small but noticeable trace of coagulated catsup along the border. Mme. Yoshoto asked me, in English—and her accent was unexpectedly charming—if I would prefer an egg, but I said, *"Non, non, madame —merci!"* I said I never ate eggs. M. Yoshoto leaned his newspaper against my water glass, and the three of us ate in silence; that is, they ate and I systematically swallowed in silence.

After breakfast, without having to leave the kitchen, M. Yoshoto put on a collarless shirt and Mme. Yoshoto took off her apron, and the three of us filed rather awkwardly downstairs to the instructors' room. There, in an untidy pile on M. Yoshoto's broad desk, lay some dozen or more unopened, enormous, bulging, Manilla envelopes. To me, they had an almost freshly brushed-and-combed look, like new pupils. M. Yoshoto assigned me to my desk, which was on the far, isolated side of the room, and asked me to be seated. Then, with Mme. Yoshoto at his side, he broke open a few of the envelopes. He and Mme. Yoshoto seemed to examine the assorted contents with some sort of method, consulting each other, now and then, in Japanese, while I sat across the room, in my blue suit and Sulka tie, trying to look simultaneously alert and patient and, somehow, indispensable to the organization. I took out a handful of soft-lead drawing pencils, from my inside jacket pocket, that I'd brought from New York with me, and laid them out, as noiselessly as possible, on the surface of my desk. Once,

M. Yoshoto glanced over at me for some reason, and I flashed him an excessively winning smile. Then, suddenly, without a word or a look in my direction, the two of them sat down at their respective desks and went to work. It was about seven-thirty.

Around nine, M. Yoshoto took off his glasses, got up and padded over to my desk with a sheaf of papers in his hand. I'd spent an hour and a half doing absolutely nothing but trying to keep my stomach from growling audibly. I quickly stood up as he came into my vicinity, stooping a trifle in order not to look disrespectfully tall. He handed me the sheaf of papers he'd brought over and asked me if I would kindly translate his written corrections from French into English. I said, *"Oui, monsieur!"* He bowed slightly, and padded back to his own desk. I pushed my handful of soft-lead drawing pencils to one side of my desk, took out my fountain pen, and fell—very nearly heartbroken—to work.

Like many a really good artist, M. Yoshoto taught drawing not a whit better than it's taught by a so-so artist who has a nice flair for teaching. With his practical overlay work—that is to say, his tracing-paper drawings imposed over the student's drawings—along with his written comments on the backs of the drawings—he was quite able to show a reasonably talented student how to draw a recognizable pig in a recognizable sty, or even a picturesque pig in a picturesque sty. But he couldn't for the life of him show anyone how to draw a beautiful pig in a beautiful sty (which, of course, was the one little technical bit his better students most greedily wanted sent to them through the mail). It was not, need I add, that he was consciously or unconsciously being frugal of his talent, or deliberately unprodigal of it, but that it simply wasn't his to give away. For me, there was no real element of surprise in this ruthless truth, and so it didn't way-lay me. But it had a certain cumulative effect, considering where I was sitting, and by the time lunch hour rolled around, I had to be very careful not to smudge my translations with the sweaty heels of my hands. As if to make things still more oppressive, M. Yoshoto's handwriting was just barely legible. At any rate, when it came time for lunch, I declined to join the Yoshotos. I said I had to go to the post office. Then I almost ran down the stairs to the street and began to walk very rapidly, with no direction at all, through a maze of strange, underprivileged-looking streets. When I came to a lunch bar, I went inside and bolted four "Coney Island Red-Hots" and three muddy cups of coffee.

On the way back to Les Amis Des Vieux Maîtres, I began to wonder, first in a familiar, faint-hearted way that I more or less knew from experience how to handle, then in an absolute panic, if there had been anything *personal* in M. Yoshoto's having used me exclusively as a translator all morning. Had old Fu Manchu known from the beginning that I was wearing, among other misleading attachments and effects, a nineteen-year-old boy's moustache? The possibility was almost unendurable to consider. It also tended to eat slowly away at my sense of justice. Here I was—a man who had won three first-prizes, a very close friend of Picasso's (which I actually was beginning to think I *was*)—being used as a translator. The punishment didn't begin to fit the crime. For one thing, my moustache, however sparse, was all mine; it hadn't been put on with spirit gum. I felt it reassuringly with my fingers as I hurried back to school. But the more I thought about the whole affair, the faster I walked, till finally I was almost trotting, as if any minute I half-expected to be stoned from all directions.

Though I'd taken only forty minutes or so for lunch, both the Yoshotos were at their desks and at work when I got back. They didn't look up or give any sign that they'd heard me come in. Perspiring and out of breath, I went over and sat down at my desk. I sat rigidly still for the next fifteen or twenty minutes, running all kinds of brand-new little Picasso anecdotes through my head, just in case M. Yoshoto suddenly got up and came over to unmask me. And, suddenly, he did get up and come over. I stood up to meet him—head on, if necessary—with a fresh little Picasso story, but, to my horror, by the time he reached me I was minus the plot. I chose the moment to express my admiration for the goose-in-flight picture hanging over Mme. Yoshoto. I praised it lavishly at some length. I said I knew a man in Paris—a very wealthy paralytic, I said—who would pay M. Yoshoto any price at all for the picture. I said I could get in touch with him immediately if M. Yoshoto was interested. Luckily, however, M. Yoshoto said the picture belonged to his cousin, who was away visiting relatives in Japan. Then, before I could express my regret, he asked me—addressing me as M. Daumier-Smith—if I would kindly correct a few lessons. He went over to his desk and returned with three enormous, bulging envelopes, and placed them on my desk. Then, while I stood dazed and incessantly nodding and feeling my jacket where my drawing pencils had been repocketed, M. Yoshoto explained to me the school's method of instruction (or, rather, its nonexistent method of instruction). After he'd returned to his own desk, it took me several minutes to pull myself together.

All three students assigned to me were English-language students. The first was a twenty-three-year-old Toronto housewife, who said her professional name was Bambi Kramer, and advised the school to address her mail accordingly. All new students at Les Amis Des Vieux Maîtres were requested to fill out questionnaire forms and to enclose photographs of themselves. Miss Kramer had enclosed a glossy, eight by ten print of herself wearing an anklet, a strapless bathing suit, and a white-duck sailor's cap. On her questionnaire form she stated that her favorite artists were Rembrandt and Walt Disney. She said she only hoped that she could some day emulate them. Her sample drawings were clipped, rather subordinately, to her photograph. All of them were arresting. One of them was unforgettable. The unforgettable one was done in florid wash colors, with a caption that read: "Forgive Them Their Trespasses." It showed three small boys fishing in an odd-looking body of water, one of their jackets draped over a "No Fishing!" sign. The tallest boy, in the foreground of the picture, appeared to have rickets in one leg and elephantiasis in the other—an effect, it was clear, that Miss Kramer had deliberately used to show that the boy was standing with his feet slightly apart.

My second student was a fifty-six-year-old "society photographer" from Windsor, Ontario, named R. Howard Ridgefield, who said that his wife had been after him for years to branch over into the painting racket. His favorite artists were Rembrandt, Sargent, and "Titan," but he added, advisedly, that he himself didn't care to draw along those lines. He said he was mostly interested in the satiric rather than the arty side of painting. To support this credo, he submitted a goodly number of original drawings and oil paintings. One of his pictures—the one I think of as his major picture—has been as recallable to me, over the years, as, say, the lyrics of "Sweet Sue" or "Let Me Call You Sweetheart." It satirized the familiar, everyday tragedy of a chaste young girl, with below-shoulder-length blond hair and udder-size breasts, being criminally assaulted in church, in the very shadow of the altar, by her minister. Both subjects' clothes were graphically in disarray. Actually, I was much less struck by the satiric implications of the picture than I was by the quality of workmanship that had gone into it. If I hadn't known they were living hundreds of miles apart, I might have sworn Ridgefield had had some purely technical help from Bambi Kramer.

Except under pretty rare circumstances, in any crisis, when I was nineteen, my funny bone invariably had the distinction of being the very first part of my body to assume partial or complete paralysis. Ridgefield and Miss Kramer did many things to me, but they didn't come at all close to amusing me. Three or four times while I was going through their envelopes, I was tempted to get up and make a formal protest to M. Yoshoto. But I had no clear idea just what sort of form my protest might take. I think I was afraid I might get over to his desk only to report, shrilly: "My mother's dead, and I have to live with her charming husband, and nobody in New York speaks French, *and there aren't any chairs in your son's room.* How do you expect me to teach these two crazy people how to draw?" In the end, being long self-trained in taking despair sitting down, I managed very easily to keep my seat. I opened my third student's envelope.

My third student was a nun of the order of Sisters of St. Joseph, named Sister Irma, who taught "cooking and drawing" at a convent elementary school just outside Toronto. And I haven't any *good* ideas concerning where to start to describe the contents of her envelope. I might just first mention that, in place of a photograph of herself, Sister Irma had enclosed, without explanation, a snapshot of her convent. It occurs to me, too, that she left blank the line in her questionnaire where the student's age was to be filled in. Otherwise, her questionnaire was filled out as perhaps no questionnaire in *this* world deserves to be filled out. She had been born and raised in Detroit, Michigan, where her father had been a "checker for Ford automobiles." Her academic education consisted of one year of high school. She had had no formal instruction in drawing. She said the only reason she was teaching it was that Sister somebody had passed on and Father Zimmermann (a name that particularly caught my eye, because it was the name of the dentist who had pulled out eight of my teeth)—Father Zimmermann had picked her to fill in. She said she had "34 kittys in my cooking class and 18 kittys in my drawing class." Her hobbies were loving her Lord and the Word of her Lord and "collecting leaves but only when they are laying right on the ground." Her favorite painter was Douglas Bunting. (A name, I don't mind saying, I've tracked down to many a blind alley, over the years.) She said her kittys always liked to "draw people when they are running and that is the one thing I am terrible at." She said she would work very hard to learn to draw better, and hoped we would not be very impatient with her.

There were, in all, only six samples of her work enclosed in the envelope. (All of her work was unsigned —a minor enough fact, but at the time, a disproportionately refreshing one. Bambi Kramer's and Ridge-

field's pictures had all been either signed or—and it
somehow seemed even more irritating—initialled.) After
thirteen years, I not only distinctly remember all six
of Sister Irma's samples, but four of them I sometimes
think I remember a trifle too distinctly for my own
peace of mind. Her best picture was done in water
colors, on brown paper. (Brown paper, especially
wrapping paper, is very pleasant, very cosy to paint
on. Many an experienced artist has used it when he
wasn't up to anything grand or grandiose.) The picture,
despite its confining size (it was about ten by twelve
inches), was a highly detailed depiction of Christ being
carried to the sepulchre in Joseph of Arimathea's garden. In the far right foreground, two men who seemed
to be Joseph's servants were rather awkwardly doing
the carrying. Joseph of Arimathea followed directly
behind them—bearing himself, under the circumstances, perhaps a trifle too erectly. At a respectably
subordinate distance behind Joseph came the women
of Galilee, mixed in with a motley, perhaps gate-crash-
ing crowd of mourners, spectators, children, and no
less than three frisky, impious mongrels. For me, the
major figure in the picture was a woman in the left
foreground, *facing* the viewer. With her right hand
raised overhead, she was frantically signalling to someone—her child, perhaps, or her husband, or possibly
the viewer—to drop everything and hurry over.
Two of the women, in the front rank of the crowd,
wore halos. Without a Bible handy, I could only make
a rough guess at their identity. But I immediately
spotted Mary Magdalene. At any rate, I was positive
I had spotted her. She was in the middle foreground,
walking apparently self-detached from the crowd, her
arms down at her sides. She wore no part of her grief,

so to speak, on her sleeve—in fact, there were no out-
ward signs at all of her late, enviable connections with
the Deceased. Her face, like all the other faces in the
picture, had been done in a cheap-priced, ready-made
flesh-tint. It was painfully clear that Sister Irma herself had found the color unsatisfactory and had tried
her unadvised, noble best to tone it down somehow.
There were no other serious flaws in the picture. None,
that is, worthy of anything but cavilling mention. It
was, in any conclusive sense, an artist's picture,
steeped in high, high, organized talent and God knows
how many hours of hard work.

One of my first reactions, of course, was to run
with Sister Irma's envelope over to M. Yoshoto. But,
once again, I kept my seat. I didn't care to risk having
Sister Irma taken away from me. At length, I just
closed her envelope with care and placed it to one
side of my desk, with the exciting plan to work on it
that night, in my own time. Then, with far more tol-
erance than I'd thought I had in me, almost with good
will, I spent the rest of the afternoon doing overlay
corrections on some male and female nudes (*sans* sex
organs) that R. Howard Ridgefield had genteely and
obscenely drawn.

Toward dinner time, I opened three buttons of my
shirt and stashed away Sister Irma's envelope where
neither thieves, nor, just to play safe, the Yoshotos,
could break in.

A tacit but iron-bound procedure covered all evening
meals at Les Amis Des Vieux Maîtres. Mme.
Yoshoto got up from her desk promptly at five-thirty
and went upstairs to prepare dinner, and Mr. Yoshoto
and I followed—fell into single file, as it were—at
six sharp. There were no side trips, however essential

or hygienic. That evening, however, with Sister Irma's envelope warm against my chest, I had never felt more relaxed. In fact, all through dinner, I couldn't have been more outgoing. I gave away a lulu of a Picasso story that had just reached me, one that I might have put aside for a rainy day. M. Yoshoto scarcely lowered his Japanese newspaper to listen to it, but Mme. Yoshoto seemed responsive, or, at least, not unresponsive. In any case, when I was finished with it, she spoke to me for the first time since she had asked me that morning if I would like an egg. She asked me if I were sure I wouldn't like a chair in my room. I said quickly, *"Non, non—merci, madame."* I said that the way the floor cushions were set right up against the wall, it gave me a good chance to practice keeping my back straight. I stood up to show her how sway-backed I was.

After dinner, while the Yoshotos were discussing, in Japanese, some perhaps provocative topic, I asked to be excused from the table. M. Yoshoto looked at me as if he weren't quite sure how I'd got into his kitchen in the first place, but nodded, and I walked quickly down the hall to my room. When I had turned on the overhead light and closed the door behind me, I took my drawing pencils out of my pocket, then took off my jacket, unbuttoned my shirt, and sat down on a floor cushion with Sister Irma's envelope in my hands. Till past four in the morning, with everything I needed spread out before me on the floor, I attended to what I thought were Sister Irma's immediate, artistic wants.

The first thing I did was to make some ten or twelve pencil sketches. Rather than go downstairs to the instructors' room for drawing paper, I drew the sketches on my personal notepaper, using both sides of the sheet. When that was done, I wrote a long, almost an endless, letter.

I've been as saving as an exceptionally neurotic magpie all my life, and I still have the next-to-the-last draft of the letter I wrote to Sister Irma that June night in 1939. I could reproduce all of it here verbatim, but it isn't necessary. I used the bulk of the letter, and I mean bulk, to suggest where and how, in her major picture, she'd run into a little trouble, especially with her colors. I listed a few artist's supplies that I thought she couldn't do without, and included approximate costs. I asked her who Douglas Bunting was. I asked where I could see some of his work. I asked her (and I knew what a long shot it was) if she had ever seen any reproductions of paintings by Antonello da Messina. I asked her to please tell me how old she was, and assured her, at great length, that the information, if given, wouldn't go beyond myself. I said the only reason that I was asking was that the information would help me to instruct her more efficiently. Virtually in the same breath, I asked if she were allowed to have visitors at her convent.

The last few lines (or cubic feet) of my letter should, I think, be reproduced here—syntax, punctuation, and all.

. . . Incidentally, if you have a command of the French language, I hope you will let me know as I am able to express myself very precisely in that language, having spent the greater part of my youth chiefly in Paris, France.

Since you are quite obviously concerned about drawing running figures, in order to convey the technique to your pupils at the Convent, I am enclosing a few sketches I have drawn myself that

may be of use. You will see that I have drawn them
rather rapidly and they are by no means perfect or
even quite commendable, but I believe they will show
you the rudiments about which you have expressed
interest. Unfortunately the director of the school
does not have any system in the method of teaching
here, I am very much afraid. I am delighted that
you are already so well advanced, but I have no
idea what he expects me to do with my other students who are very retarded and chiefly stupid, in
my opinion.

Unfortunately, I am an agnostic; however, I am
quite an admirer of St. Francis of Assisi from a distance, it goes without saying. I wonder if perhaps
you are thoroughly acquainted with what he (St.
Francis of Assisi) said when they were about to
cauterise one of his eyeballs with a red-hot, burning iron? He said as follows: "Brother Fire, God
made you beautiful and strong and useful; I pray
you be courteous to me." You paint slightly the way
he spoke, in many pleasant ways, in my opinion.
Incidentally, may I ask if the young lady in the
foreground in the blue outfit is Mary Magdalene?
I mean in the picture we have been discussing, of
course. If she is not, I have been sadly deluding myself. However, this is no novelty.

I hope you will consider me entirely at your
disposal as long as you are a student at Les Amis
Des Vieux Maîtres. Frankly, I think you are greatly
talented and would not even be slightly startled if
you developed into a genius before many years
have gone by. I would not falsely encourage you in
this matter. That is one reason why I asked you if
the young lady in the foreground in the blue outfit was Mary Magdalene, because if it was, you were
using your incipient genius somewhat more than
your religious inclinations, I am afraid. However, this
is nothing to fear, in my opinion.

With sincere hope that you are enjoying completely perfect health, I am,
Very respectfully yours,
(signed)
JEAN DE DAUMIER-SMITH
Staff Instructor
Les Amis Des Vieux Maîtres

P.S. I have nearly forgotten that students are supposed to submit envelopes every second Monday to the school. For your first assignment will you kindly make some outdoor sketches for me? Do them very freely and do not strain. I am unaware, of course, how much time they give you for your personal drawing at your Convent and hope you will advise me. Also I beg you to buy those necessary supplies I took the liberty of advocating, as I would like you to begin using oils as soon as possible. If you will pardon my saying so, I believe you are too passionate to paint just in watercolors and never in oils indefinitely. I say that quite impersonally and do not mean to be obnoxious; actually, it is intended as a compliment. Also please send me *all* of your old former work that you have on hand, as I am eager to see it. The days will be insufferable for me till your next envelope arrives, it goes without saying.

If it is not overstepping myself, I would greatly appreciate your telling me if you find being a nun very satisfactory, in a spiritual way, of course. Frankly, I have been studying various religions as a hobby ever since I read volumes 36, 44, 45 of the *Harvard Classics,* which you may be acquainted with. I am especially delighted with Martin Luther, who was a Protestant, of course. Please do not be offended by this. I advocate no doctrine; it is not my nature to do so. As a last thought, please do not forget to advise me as to your visiting hours, as my weekends are free as far as I know and I may happen to be in your environs some Saturday by chance. Also please do not forget to inform me if you have a reasonable command of the French language, as for all intents and purposes I am comparatively speechless in English owing to my varied and largely insensible upbringing.

I mailed my letter and drawings to Sister Irma around three-thirty in the morning, going out to the street to do it. Then, literally overjoyed, I undressed myself with thick fingers and fell into bed.

Just before I fell asleep, the moaning sound again came through the wall from the Yoshotos' bedroom. I pictured both Yoshotos coming to me in the morning and asking me, begging me, to hear their secret problem out, to the last, terrible detail. I saw exactly how it would be. I would sit down between them at the kitchen table and listen to each of them. I would listen, listen, listen, with my head in my hands—till finally, unable to stand it any longer, I would reach down into Mme. Yoshoto's throat, take up her heart in my hand and warm it as I would a bird. Then, when all was put right, I would show Sister Irma's work to the Yoshotos, and they would share my joy.

The fact is always obvious much too late, but the most singular difference between happiness and joy is that happiness is a solid and joy a liquid. Mine started to seep through its container as early as the next morning, when M. Yoshoto dropped by at my desk with the envelopes of two new students. I was working on Bambi Kramer's drawings at the time, and quite spleenlessly, knowing as I did that my letter to Sister Irma was safely in the mail. But I was nowhere even nearly prepared to face the freakish fact that there were two people in the world who had less talent for drawing than either Bambi or R. Howard Ridgefield. Feeling virtue go out of me, I lit a cigarette in the instructors' room for the first time since I'd joined the staff. It seemed to help, and I turned back to Bambi's work. But before I'd taken more than three or four drags, I felt, without actually glancing up and over, that M. Yoshoto was looking at me. Then, for confirmation, I heard his chair being pushed back. As usual, I got up to meet him when he came over. He explained to me, in a bloody irritating whisper, that he personally had no objection to smoking, but that, alas, the school's policy was against smoking in the instructors' room. He cut short my profuse apologies with a magnanimous wave of his hand, and went back over to his and Mme. Yoshoto's side of the room. I wondered, in a real panic, how I would manage to get sanely through the next thirteen days to the Monday when Sister Irma's next envelope was due.

That was Tuesday morning. I spent the rest of the working day and all the working portions of the next two days keeping myself feverishly busy. I took all of Bambi Kramer's and R. Howard Ridgefield's drawings apart, as it were, and put them together with brand-new parts. I designed for both of them literally dozens of insulting, subnormal, but quite constructive, drawing exercises. I wrote long letters to them. I almost begged R. Howard Ridgefield to give up his satire for a while. I asked Bambi, with maximum delicacy, to please hold off, temporarily, submitting any more drawings with titles kindred to "Forgive Them Their Trespasses." Then, Thursday mid-afternoon, feeling good and jumpy, I started in on one of the two new students, an American from Bangor, Maine, who said in his questionnaire, with wordy, Honest-John integrity, that he was his own favorite artist. He referred to himself as a realist-abstractionist. As for my after-school hours, Tuesday evening I took a bus into Montreal proper and sat through a Cartoon Festival Week program at a third-rate movie house—which largely entailed being a witness to a succession of cats being bombarded with champagne corks by mice gangs. Wednesday evening, I gathered up the floor cushions in my room, piled them three high, and tried to sketch from memory Sister Irma's picture of Christ's burial.

I'm tempted to say that Thursday evening was peculiar, or perhaps macabre, but the fact is, I have no bill-filling adjectives for Thursday evening. I left Les Amis after dinner and went I don't know where—perhaps to a movie, perhaps for just a long walk; I can't remember, and, for once, my diary for 1939 lets me down, too, for the page I need is a total blank.

I know, though, why the page is a blank. As I was returning from wherever I'd spent the evening—and I do remember that it was after dark—I stopped on the sidewalk outside the school and looked into the lighted display window of the orthopedic appliances shop. Then something altogether hideous happened. The thought was forced on me that no matter how coolly or sensibly or gracefully I might one day learn to live my life, I would always at best be a visitor in a garden of enamel urinals and bedpans, with a sightless, wooden dummy-deity standing by in a marked-down rupture truss. The thought, certainly, couldn't have been endurable for more than a few seconds. I remember fleeing upstairs to my room and getting undressed and into bed without so much as opening my diary, much less making an entry.

I lay awake for hours, shivering. I listened to the moaning in the next room and I thought, forcibly, of my star pupil. I tried to visualize the day I would visit her at her convent. I saw her coming to meet me—near a high, wire fence—a shy, beautiful girl of eighteen who had not yet taken her final vows and was still free to go out into the world with the Peter Abelard-type man of her choice. I saw us walking slowly, silently, toward a far, verdant part of the convent grounds, where suddenly, and without sin, I would put my arm around her waist. The image was too ecstatic to hold in place, and, finally, I let go, and fell asleep.

I spent all of Friday morning and most of the afternoon at hard labor trying, with the use of overlay tissue, to make recognizable trees out of a forest of phallic symbols the man from Bangor, Maine, had consciously drawn on expensive linen paper. Mentally, spiritually, and physically, I was feeling pretty torpid along toward four-thirty in the afternoon, and I only half stood up when M. Yoshoto came over to my desk for an instant. He handed something to me —handed it to me as impersonally as the average waiter distributes menus. It was a letter from the Mother Superior of Sister Irma's convent, informing M. Yoshoto that Father Zimmermann, through circumstances outside his control, was forced to alter his decision to allow Sister Irma to study at Les Amis Des Vieux Maîtres. The writer said she deeply regretted any inconveniences or confusions this change of plans might cause the school. She sincerely hoped that the first tuition payment of fourteen dollars might be refunded to the diocese.

The mouse, I've been sure for years, limps home from the site of the burning ferris wheel with a brand-new, airtight plan for killing the cat. After I'd read and reread and then, for great, long minutes, stared at the Mother Superior's letter, I suddenly broke away from it and wrote letters to my four remaining students, advising them to give up the idea of becoming artists. I told them, individually, that they had absolutely no talent worth developing and that they were simply wasting their own valuable time as well as the school's. I wrote all four letters in French. When I was finished, I immediately went out and mailed them. The satisfaction was short-lived, but very, very good while it lasted.

When it came time to join the parade to the kitchen for dinner, I asked to be excused. I said I wasn't feeling well. (I lied, in 1939, with far greater conviction than I told the truth—so I was positive that M. Yoshoto looked at me with suspicion when I said I wasn't feeling well.) Then I went up to my room and sat down on a cushion. I sat there for surely an hour, staring at a daylit hole in the window blind, without smoking or taking off my coat or loosening my necktie. Then, abruptly, I got up and brought over a quantity of my personal notepaper and wrote a second letter to Sister Irma, using the floor as a desk.

I never mailed the letter. The following reproduction is copied straight from the original.

Montreal, Canada
June 28, 1939

DEAR SISTER IRMA,
Did I, by chance, say anything obnoxious or ir-

reverent to you in my last letter that reached the attention of Father Zimmermann and caused you discomfort in some way? If this is the case, I beg you to give me at least a reasonable chance to retract whatever it was I may have unwittingly said in my ardor to become friends with you as well as student and teacher. Is this asking too much? I do not believe it is.

The bare truth is as follows: If you do not learn a few more rudiments of the profession, you will only be a very, very interesting artist the rest of your life instead of a great one. This is terrible, in my opinion. Do you realize how grave the situation is?

It is possible that Father Zimmermann made you resign from the school because he thought it might interfere with your being a competent nun. If this is the case, I cannot avoid saying that I think it was very rash of him in more ways than one. It would not interfere with your being a nun. I live like an evil-minded monk myself. The worst that being an artist could do to you would be that it would make you slightly unhappy constantly. However, this is not a tragic situation, in my opinion. The happiest day of my life was many years ago when I was seventeen. I was on my way for lunch to meet my mother, who was going out on the street for the first time after a long illness, and I was feeling ecstatically happy when suddenly, as I was coming in to the Avenue Victor Hugo, which is a street in Paris, I bumped into a chap without any nose. I ask you to please consider that factor, in fact I beg you. It is quite pregnant with meaning.

It is also possible that Father Zimmermann caused you to stop matriculating for the reason perhaps that your convent lacks funds to pay the tuition. I frankly hope this is the case, not only because it relieves my mind, but in a practical sense. If this is indeed the case, you have only to say the word and I will offer my services gratis for an indefinite period of time. Can we discuss this matter further? May I ask again when your visiting days at the convent are? May I be free to plan to visit you at the convent next Saturday afternoon, July 6, between 3 and 5 o'clock in the afternoon, dependent upon the schedule of trains between Montreal and Toronto? I await your reply with great anxiety.

> With respect and admiration,
> Sincerely yours,
> (signed)
> JEAN DE DAUMIER-SMITH
> *Staff Instructor*
> *Les Amis Des Vieux Maîtres*

P.S. In my last letter I casually asked if the young lady in the blue outfit in the foreground of your religious picture was Mary Magdalene, the sinner. If you have not as yet replied to my letter, please go on refraining. It is possible that I was mistaken and I do not willfully invite any disillusions at this point in my life. I am willing to stay in the dark.

Even today, as late as *now,* I have a tendency to wince when I remember that I brought a dinner suit up to Les Amis with me. But bring one I did, and after I'd finished my letter to Sister Irma, I put it on. The whole affair seemed to call out for my getting drunk, and since I had never in my life been drunk (for fear that excessive drinking would shake the hand that painted the pictures that copped the three first prizes, etc.), I felt compelled to dress for the tragic occasion.

While the Yoshotos were still in the kitchen, I slipped downstairs and telephoned the Windsor Hotel

—which Bobby's friend, Mrs. X, had recommended to me before I'd left New York. I reserved a table for one, for eight o'clock.

Around seven-thirty, dressed and slicked up, I stuck my head outside my door to see if either of the Yoshotos were on the prowl. I didn't want them to see me in my dinner jacket, for some reason. They weren't in sight, and I hurried down to the street and began to look for a cab. My letter to Sister Irma was in the inside pocket of my jacket. I intended to read it over at dinner, preferably by candlelight.

I walked block after block without so much as seeing a cab at all, let alone an empty one. It was rough going. The Verdun section of Montreal was in no sense a dressy neighborhood, and I was convinced that every passer-by was giving me a second, basically censorious look. When, finally, I came to the lunch bar where I'd bolted the "Coney Island Red-Hots" on Monday, I decided to let my reservation at the Hotel Windsor go by the board. I went into the lunch bar, sat down in an end booth, and kept my left hand over my black tie while I ordered soup, rolls and black coffee. I hoped that the other patrons would think I was a waiter on his way to work.

While I was on my second cup of coffee, I took out my unmailed letter to Sister Irma and reread it. The substance of it seemed to me a trifle thin, and I decided to hurry back to Les Amis and touch it up a bit. I also thought over my plans to visit Sister Irma, and wondered if it might not be a good idea to pick up my train reservations later that same evening. With those two thoughts in mind—neither of which really gave me the sort of lift I needed—I left the lunch bar and walked rapidly back to school.

Something extremely out of the way happened to me some fifteen minutes later. A statement, I'm aware, that has all the unpleasant earmarks of a build-up, but quite the contrary is true. I'm about to touch on an extraordinary experience, one that still strikes me as having been quite transcendent, and I'd like, if possible, to avoid seeming to pass it off as a case, or even a borderline case, of genuine mysticism. (To do otherwise, I feel, would be tantamount to implying or stating that the difference in spiritual *sorties* between St. Francis and the average, highstrung, Sunday leper-kisser is *only* a vertical one.)

In the nine o'clock twilight, as I approached the school building from across the street, there was a light on in the orthopedic appliances shop. I was startled to see a live person in the shopcase, a hefty girl of about thirty, in a green, yellow and lavender chiffon dress. She was changing the truss on the wooden dummy. As I came up to the show window, she had evidently just taken off the old truss; it was under her left arm (her right "profile" was toward me), and she was lacing up the new one on the dummy. I stood watching her, fascinated, till suddenly she sensed, then saw, that she was being watched. I quickly smiled—to show her that this was a non-hostile figure in the tuxedo in the twilight on the other side of the glass—but it did no good. The girl's confusion was out of all normal proportion. She blushed, she dropped the removed truss, she stepped back on a stack of irrigation basins—and her feet went out from under her. I reached out to her instantly, hitting the tips of my fingers on the glass. She landed heavily on her bottom, like a skater. She immediately got to her feet without looking at me. Her face still flushed, she pushed her hair back with one hand, and resumed lacing up the truss on the dummy. It was just then that I had my Experience. Suddenly (and I say this, I believe, with all due self-consciousness), the sun came up and sped toward the bridge of my nose at the rate of ninety-three million miles a second. Blinded and very frightened—I had to put my hand on the glass to keep my balance. The thing lasted for no more than a few seconds. When I got my sight back, the girl had gone from the window, leaving behind her a shimmering field of exquisite, twice-blessed, enamel flowers.

I backed away from the window and walked around the block twice, till my knees stopped buckling. Then, without daring to venture another look into the shop window, I went upstairs to my room and lay down on my bed. Some minutes, or hours later, I made, in French, the following brief entry in my diary: "I am giving Sister Irma her freedom to follow her own destiny. Everybody is a nun." (*Tout le monde est une nonne.*)

Before going to bed for the night, I wrote letters to my four just-expelled students, reinstating them. I said a mistake had been made in the administration department. Actually, the letters seemed to write themselves. It may have had something to do with the fact that, before sitting down to write, I'd brought a chair up from downstairs.

It seems altogether anticlimactic to mention it, but Les Amis Des Vieux Maîtres closed down less than a week later, for being improperly licensed (for not being licensed at *all*, as a matter of fact). I packed up and joined Bobby, my stepfather, in Rhode Island, where I spent the next six or eight weeks, till art school reopened, investigating that most interesting of all summer-active animals, the American Girl in Shorts.

Right or wrong, I never again got in touch with Sister Irma.

Occasionally, I still hear from Bambi Kramer, though. The last I heard, she'd branched over into designing her own Christmas cards. They'll be something to see, if she hasn't lost her touch.

Teddy

I 'LL EXQUISITE DAY *you,* buddy, if you don't get down
off that bag this minute. And I mean it," Mr. Mc-
Ardle said. He was speaking from the inside twin bed
—the bed farther away from the porthole. Viciously,
with more of a whimper than a sigh, he foot-pushed
his top sheet clear of his ankles, as though any kind
of coverlet was suddenly too much for his sunburned,
debilitated-looking body to bear. He was lying supine,
in just the trousers of his pajamas, a lighted cigarette
in his right hand. His head was propped up just
enough to rest uncomfortably, almost masochistically,
against the very base of the headboard. His pillow
and ashtray were both on the floor, between his and
Mrs. McArdle's bed. Without raising his body, he
reached out a nude, inflamed-pink, right arm and
flicked his ashes in the general direction of the night
table. "October, for God's sake," he said. "If this is
October weather, gimme August." He turned his head
to the right again, toward Teddy, looking for trouble.
"C'mon," he said. "What the hell do you think I'm
talking for? My health? Get *down* off there, please."

Teddy was standing on the broadside of a new-looking cowhide Gladstone, the better to see out of his parents' open porthole. He was wearing extremely dirty, white ankle-sneakers, no socks, seersucker shorts that were both too long for him and at least a size too large in the seat, an overly laundered T shirt that had a hole the size of a dime in the right shoulder, and an incongruously handsome, black alligator belt. He needed a haircut—especially at the nape of the neck—the worst way, as only a small boy with an almost full-grown head and a reedlike neck can need one.

"Teddy, did you hear me?"

Teddy was not leaning out of the porthole quite so far or so precariously as small boys are apt to lean out of open portholes—both his feet, in fact, were flat on the surface of the Gladstone—but neither was he just conservatively well-tipped; his face was considerably more outside than inside the cabin. Nonetheless, he was well within hearing of his father's voice—his father's voice, that is, most singularly. Mr. McArdle played leading roles on no fewer than three daytime radio serials when he was in New York, and he had what might be called a third-class leading man's speaking voice: narcissistically deep and resonant, functionally prepared at a moment's notice to out-male anyone in the same room with it, if necessary even a small boy. When it was on vacation from its professional chores, it fell, as a rule, alternately in love with sheer volume and a theatrical brand of quietness-steadiness. Right now, volume was in order.

"*Teddy.* God damn it—did you hear me?"

Teddy turned around at the waist, without changing the vigilant position of his feet on the Gladstone, and gave his father a look of inquiry, whole and pure. His eyes, which were pale brown in color, and not at all large, were slightly crossed—the left eye more than the right. They were not crossed enough to be disfiguring, or even to be necessarily noticeable at first glance. They were crossed just enough to be mentioned, and only in context with the fact that one might have thought long and seriously before wishing them straighter, or deeper, or browner, or wider set. His face, just as it was, carried the impact, however oblique and slow-travelling, of real beauty.

"I want you to get down off that bag, now. How many times do you want me to tell you?" Mr. Mc-Ardle said.

"Stay exactly where you are, darling," said Mrs. McArdle, who evidently had a little trouble with her sinuses early in the morning. Her eyes were open, but only just. "Don't move the tiniest part of an inch." She was lying on her right side, her face, on the pillow, turned left, toward Teddy and the porthole, her back to her husband. Her second sheet was drawn tight over her very probably nude body, enclosing her, arms and all, up to the chin. "Jump up and down," she said, and closed her eyes. "Crush Daddy's bag."

"That's a Jesus-brilliant thing to say," Mr. Mc-Ardle said quietly-steadily, addressing the back of his wife's head. "I pay twenty-two pounds for a bag, and I ask the boy civilly not to stand on it, and you tell him to jump up and down on it. What's that supposed to be? Funny?"

"If that bag can't support a ten-year-old boy, who's thirteen pounds underweight for his age, I don't want it in my cabin," Mrs. McArdle said, without opening her eyes.

"You know what I'd like to do?" Mr. McArdle said. "I'd like to kick your goddam head open."

"Why don't you?"

Mr. McArdle abruptly propped himself up on one elbow and squashed out his cigarette stub on the glass top of the night table. "One of these days—" he began grimly.

"One of these days, you're going to have a tragic, tragic heart attack," Mrs. McArdle said, with a minimum of energy. Without bringing her arms into the open, she drew her top sheet more tightly around and under her body. "There'll be a small, tasteful funeral, and everybody's going to ask who that attractive woman in the red dress is, sitting there in the first row, flirting with the organist and making a holy—"

"You're so goddam funny it isn't even funny," Mr. McArdle said, lying inertly on his back again.

During this little exchange, Teddy had faced around and resumed looking out of the porthole. "We passed the *Queen Mary* at three-thirty-two this morning, going the other way, if anybody's interested," he said slowly. "Which I doubt." His voice was oddly and beautifully rough cut, as some small boys' voices are. Each of his phrasings was rather like a little ancient island, inundated by a miniature sea of whiskey. "That deck steward Booper despises had it on his blackboard."

"I'll *Queen Mary you,* buddy, if you don't get off that bag this minute," his father said. He turned his head toward Teddy. "Get *down* from there, now. Go get yourself a haircut or something." He looked at the back of his wife's head again. "He looks precocious, for God's sake."

"I haven't any money," Teddy said. He placed his hands more securely on the sill of the porthole, and lowered his chin onto the backs of his fingers. "Mother. You know that man who sits right next to us in the dining room? Not the very thin one. The other one, at the same table. Right next to where our waiter puts his tray down."

"Mm-hmm," Mrs. McArdle said. "Teddy. Darling. Let Mother sleep just five minutes more, like a sweet boy."

"Wait just a second. This is quite interesting," Teddy said, without raising his chin from its resting place and without taking his eyes off the ocean. "He was in the gym a little while ago, while Sven was weighing me. He came up and started talking to me. He heard that last tape I made. Not the one in April. The one in May. He was at a party in Boston just before he went to Europe, and somebody at the party knew somebody in the Leidekker examining group—he didn't say who—and they borrowed that last tape I made and played it at the party. He seems very interested in it. He's a friend of Professor Babcock's. Apparently he's a teacher himself. He said he was at Trinity College in Dublin, all summer."

"Oh?" said Mrs. McArdle. "At a *party* they played it?" She lay gazing sleepily at the backs of Teddy's legs.

"I guess so," Teddy said. "He told Sven quite a bit about me, right while I was standing there. It was rather embarrassing."

"Why should it be embarrassing?"

Teddy hesitated. "I said 'rather' embarrassing. I qualified it."

"I'll qualify *you,* buddy, if you don't get the hell off that bag," Mr. McArdle said. He had just lit a fresh cigarette. "I'm going to count three. *One,* God damn it . . . *Two . . .*"

"What time is it?" Mrs. McArdle suddenly asked

the backs of Teddy's legs. "Don't you and Booper have a swimming lesson at ten-thirty?"

"We have time," Teddy said. "—Vloom!" He suddenly thrust his whole head out of the porthole, kept it there a few seconds, then brought it in just long enough to report, "Someone just dumped a whole garbage can of orange peels out the window."

"Out the window. Out the *window*," Mr. McArdle said sarcastically, flicking his ashes. "Out the porthole, buddy, out the porthole." He glanced over at his wife. "Call Boston. Quick, get the Leidekker examining group on the phone."

"Oh, you're such a brilliant wit," Mrs. McArdle said. "Why do you try?"

Teddy took in most of his head. "They float very nicely," he said without turning around. "That's interesting."

"Teddy. For the last time. I'm going to count three, and then I'm—"

"I don't mean it's interesting that they float," Teddy said. "It's interesting that I know about them being there. If I hadn't seen them, then I wouldn't know they were there, and if I didn't know they were there, I wouldn't be able to say that they even exist. That's a very nice, perfect example of the way—"

"Teddy," Mrs. McArdle interrupted, without visibly stirring under her top sheet. "Go find Booper for me. Where is she? I don't want her lolling around in that sun again today, with that burn."

"She's adequately covered. I made her wear her dungarees," Teddy said. "Some of them are starting to sink now. In a few minutes, the only place they'll still be floating will be inside my mind. That's quite interesting, because if you look at it a certain way, that's where they started floating in the first place. If I'd never been standing here at all, or if somebody'd come along and sort of chopped my head off right while I was—"

"Where is she now?" Mrs. McArdle asked. "Look at Mother a minute, Teddy."

Teddy turned and looked at his mother. "What?" he said.

"Where's Booper now? I don't want her meandering all around the deck chairs again, bothering people. If that awful man—"

"She's all right. I gave her the camera."

Mr. McArdle lurched up on one arm. "You gave her the *cam*era!" he said. "What the hell's the idea? My goddam Leica! I'm not going to have a six-year-old child gallivanting all over—"

"I showed her how to hold it so she won't drop it," Teddy said. "And I took the film out, naturally."

"I want that camera, Teddy. You hear me? I want you to get down off that bag this minute, and I want that camera back in this room in *five minutes*—or there's going to be one little genius among the missing. Is that clear?"

Teddy turned his feet around on the Gladstone, and stepped down. He bent over and tied the lace of his left sneaker while his father, still raised up on one elbow, watched him like a monitor.

"Tell Booper I want her," Mrs. McArdle said. "And give Mother a kiss."

Finished tying his sneaker lace, Teddy perfunctorily gave his mother a kiss on the cheek. She in turn brought her left arm out from under the sheet, as if bent on encircling Teddy's waist with it, but by the time she had got it out from under, Teddy had moved on. He had come around the other side and entered the space between the two beds. He stooped, and stood up with his father's pillow under his left arm and the glass ashtray that belonged on the night table in his right hand. Switching the ashtray over to his left hand, he went up to the night table and, with the edge of his right hand, swept his father's cigarette stubs and ashes into the ashtray. Then, before putting the ashtray back where it belonged, he used the under side of his forearm to wipe off the filmy wake of ashes from the glass top of the table. He wiped off his forearm on his seersucker shorts. Then he placed the ashtray on the glass top, with a world of care, as if he believed an ashtray should be dead-centered on the surface of a night table or not placed at all. At that point, his father, who had been watching him, abruptly gave up watching him. "Don't you want your pillow?" Teddy asked him.

"I want that camera, young man."

"You can't be very comfortable in that position. It isn't possible," Teddy said. "I'll leave it right here." He placed the pillow on the foot of the bed, clear of his father's feet. He started out of the cabin.

"Teddy," his mother said, without turning over. "Tell Booper I want to see her before her swimming lesson."

"Why don't you leave the kid alone?" Mr. McArdle asked. "You seem to resent her having a few lousy minutes' freedom. You know how you treat her? I'll tell you exactly how you treat her. You treat her like a bloomin' criminal."

"Bloomin'! Oh, that's cute! You're getting so English, lover."

Teddy lingered for a moment at the door, reflectively experimenting with the door handle, turning it slowly left and right. "After I go out this door, I may only exist in the minds of all my acquaintances," he said. "I may be an orange peel."

"What, darling?" Mrs. McArdle asked from across the cabin, still lying on her right side.

"Let's get on the ball, buddy. Let's get that Leica down here."

"Come give Mother a kiss. A nice, big one."

"Not right now," Teddy said absently. "I'm tired." He closed the door behind him.

The ship's daily newspaper lay just outside the door-sill. It was a single sheet of glossy paper, with printing on just one side. Teddy picked it up and began to read it as he started slowly aft down the long passageway. From the opposite end, a huge, blond woman in a starched white uniform was coming toward him, carrying a vase of long-stemmed, red roses. As she passed Teddy, she put out her left hand and grazed the top of his head with it, saying, "Somebody needs a haircut!" Teddy passively looked up from his newspaper, but the woman had passed, and he didn't look back. He went on reading. At the end of the passageway, before an enormous mural of Saint George and the Dragon over the staircase landing, he folded the ship's newspaper into quarters and put it into his left hip pocket. He then climbed the broad, shallow, carpeted steps up to Main Deck, one flight up. He took two steps at a time, but slowly, holding on to the banister, putting his whole body into it, as if the act of climbing a flight of stairs was for him, as it is for many children, a moderately pleasurable end in itself. At the Main Deck landing, he went directly over to the Purser's desk, where a good-looking girl in naval uniform was presiding at the moment. She was stapling some mimeographed sheets of paper together.

"Can you tell me what time that game starts today, please?" Teddy asked her.

"I beg your pardon?"

"Can you tell me what time that game starts today?"

The girl gave him a lipsticky smile. "What game, honey?" she asked.

"You know. That word game they had yesterday and the day before, where you're supposed to supply the missing words. It's mostly that you have to put everything in context."

The girl held off fitting three sheets of paper between the planes of her stapler. "Oh," she said. "Not till late afternoon, I believe. I believe it's around four o'clock. Isn't that a little over your head, dear?"

"No, it isn't . . . Thank you," Teddy said, and started to leave.

"Wait a minute, honey! What's your name?"

"Theodore McArdle," Teddy said. "What's yours?"

"My name?" said the girl, smiling. "My name's Ensign Mathewson."

Teddy watched her press down on her stapler. "I knew you were an ensign," he said. "I'm not sure, but I believe when somebody asks your name you're supposed to say your whole name. Jane Mathewson, or Phyllis Mathewson, or whatever the case may be."

"Oh, *really*?"

"As I say, I *think* so," Teddy said. "I'm not sure, though. It may be different if you're in uniform. Anyway, thank you for the information. Goodbye!" He turned and took the stairs up to the Promenade Deck, again two at a time, but this time as if in rather a hurry.

He found Booper, after some extensive looking, high up on the Sports Deck. She was in a sunny clearing—a glade, almost—between two deck-tennis courts that were not in use. In a squatting position, with the sun at her back and a light breeze riffling her silky, blond hair, she was busily piling twelve or fourteen shuffleboard discs into two tangent stacks, one for the black discs, one for the red. A very small boy, in a cotton sun suit, was standing close by, on her right, purely in an observer's capacity. "Look!" Booper said commandingly to her brother as he approached. She sprawled forward and surrounded the two stacks of shuffleboard discs with her arms to show off her accomplishment, to isolate it from whatever else was aboard ship. *"My*ron," she said hostilely, addressing her companion, "you're making it all shadowy, so my brother can't see. Move your carcass." She shut her eyes and waited, with a cross-bearing grimace, till Myron moved.

Teddy stood over the two stacks of discs and looked down appraisingly at them. "That's very nice," he said. "Very symmetrical."

"This guy," Booper said, indicating Myron, "never even heard of *back*gammon. They don't even have one."

Teddy glanced briefly, objectively, at Myron. "Listen," he said to Booper. "Where's the camera? Daddy wants it right away."

"He doesn't even live in New York," Booper informed Teddy. "And his father's dead. He was killed in Korea." She turned to Myron. "Wasn't he?" she demanded, but without waiting for a response. "Now if his mother dies, he'll be an orphan. He didn't even know that." She looked at Myron. *"Did* you?"

Myron, non-committal, folded his arms.

"You're the stupidest person I ever met," Booper said to him. "You're the stupidest person in this ocean. Did you know that?"

"He is not," Teddy said. "You are not, Myron." He addressed his sister: "Give me your attention a second. Where's the camera? I have to have it immediately. Where is it?"

"Over there," Booper said, indicating no direction at all. She drew her two stacks of shuffleboard discs in closer to her. "All I need now is two giants," she said. "They could play backgammon till they got all tired and then they could climb up on that smokestack and throw these at everybody and kill them." She looked at Myron. "They could kill your perents," she said to him knowledgeably. "And if that didn't kill them, you know what you could do? You could put some poison on some marshmellows and make them eat it."

The Leica was about ten feet away, next to the white railing that surrounded the Sports Deck. It lay in the drain gully, on its side. Teddy went over and picked it up by its strap and hung it around his neck. Then, immediately, he took it off. He took it over to Booper. "Booper, do me a favor. You take it down, please," he said. "It's ten o'clock. I have to write in my diary."

"I'm busy."

"Mother wants to see you right away, anyway," Teddy said.

"You're a liar."

"I'm not a liar. She does," Teddy said. "So please take this down with you when you go . . . C'mon, Booper."

"What's she want to see me for?" Booper demanded. "I don't want to see *her*." She suddenly struck Myron's hand, which was in the act of picking off the top shuffleboard disc from the red stack. "Hands off," she said.

Teddy

Teddy hung the strap attached to the Leica around her neck. "I'm serious, now. Take this down to Daddy right away, and then I'll see you at the pool later on," he said. "I'll meet you right at the pool at ten-thirty. Or right outside that place where you change your clothes. Be on time, now. It's way down on E Deck, don't forget, so leave yourself plenty of time." He turned, and left.

"I hate you! I hate everybody in this ocean!" Booper called after him.

Below the Sports Deck, on the broad, after end of the Sun Deck, uncompromisingly alfresco, were some seventy-five or more deck chairs, set up and aligned seven or eight rows deep, with aisles just wide enough for the deck steward to use without unavoidably tripping over the sunning passengers' paraphernalia—knitting bags, dust-jacketed novels, bottles of sun-tan lotion, cameras. The area was crowded when Teddy arrived. He started at the rearmost row and moved methodically, from row to row, stopping at each chair, whether or not it was occupied, to read the name placard on its arm. Only one or two of the reclining passengers spoke to him—that is, made any of the commonplace pleasantries adults are sometimes prone to make to a ten-year-old boy who is single-mindedly looking for the chair that belongs to him. His youngness and single-mindedness were obvious enough, but perhaps his general demeanor altogether lacked, or had too little of, that sort of cute solemnity that many adults readily speak up, or down, to. His clothes may have had something to do with it, too. The hole in the shoulder of his T shirt was not a cute hole. The excess material in the seat of his seersucker shorts, the excess length of the shorts themselves, were not cute excesses.

Teddy

The McArdles' four deck chairs, cushioned and ready for occupancy, were situated in the middle of the second row from the front. Teddy sat down in one of them so that—whether or not it was his intention —no one was sitting directly on either side of him. He stretched out his bare, unsuntanned legs, feet together, on the leg rest, and, almost simultaneously, took a small, ten-cent notebook out of his right hip pocket. Then, with instantly one-pointed concentration, as if only he and the notebook existed—no sunshine, no fellow passengers, no ship—he began to turn the pages.

With the exception of a very few pencil notations, the entries in the notebook had apparently all been made with a ball-point pen. The handwriting itself was manuscript style, such as is currently being taught in American schools, instead of the old, Palmer method. It was legible without being pretty-pretty. The flow was what was remarkable about the handwriting. In no sense—no mechanical sense, at any rate—did the words and sentences look as though they had been written by a child.

Teddy gave considerable reading time to what looked like his most recent entry. It covered a little more than three pages:

Diary for October 27, 1952
Property of Theodore McArdle
412 A Deck

Appropriate and pleasant reward if finder promptly returns to Theodore McArdle.

See if you can find daddy's army dog tags and

wear them whenever possible. It won't kill you and he will like it.

Answer Professor Mandell's letter when you get a chance and the patience. Ask him not to send me any more poetry books. I already have enough for 1 year anyway. I am quite sick of it anyway. A man walks along the beach and unfortunately gets hit in the head by a cocoanut. His head unfortunately cracks open in two halves. Then his wife comes along the beach singing a song and sees the 2 halves and recognizes them and picks them up. She gets very sad of course and cries heart break-ingly. That is exactly where I am tired of poetry. Supposing the lady just picks up the 2 halves and shouts into them very angrily "Stop that!" Do not mention this when you answer his letter, however. It is quite controversial and Mrs. Mandell is a poet besides.

Get Sven's address in Elizabeth, New Jersey. It would be interesting to meet his wife, also his dog Lindy. However, I would not like to own a dog myself.

Write condolence letter to Dr. Wokawara about his nephritis. Get his new address from mother.

Try the sports deck for meditation tomorrow morning before breakfast but do not lose con-sciousness. Also do not lose consciousness in the dining room if that waiter drops that big spoon again. Daddy was quite furious.

Words and expressions to look up in library to-morrow when you return the books—

nephritis
myriad

Teddy

gift horse
cunning
triumvirate

Be nicer to librarian. Discuss some general things with him when he gets kittenish.

Teddy abruptly took out a small, bullet-shaped, ballpoint pen from the side pocket of his shorts, uncapped it, and began to write. He used his right thigh as a desk, instead of the chair arm.

Diary for October 28, 1952
Same address and reward as written on October 26 and 27, 1952.

I wrote letters to the following persons after meditation this morning.

> Dr. Wokawara
> Professor Mandell
> Professor Peet
> Burgess Hake, Jr.
> Roberta Hake
> Sanford Hake
> Grandma Hake
> Mr. Graham
> Professor Walton

I could have asked mother where daddy's dog tags are but she would probably say I don't have to wear them. I know he has them with him because I saw him pack them.

Life is a gift horse in my opinion.

I think it is very tasteless of Professor Walton to criticize my parents. He wants people to be a certain way.

Teddy

It will either happen today or February 14, 1958
when I am sixteen. It is ridiculous to mention
even.

After making this last entry, Teddy continued to
keep his attention on the page and his ball-point pen
poised, as though there were more to come.

He apparently was unaware that he had a lone interested observer. About fifteen feet forwardship from
the first row of deck chairs, and eighteen or twenty
rather sun-blinding feet overhead, a young man was
steadily watching him from the Sports Deck railing.
This had been going on for some ten minutes. It was
evident that the young man was now reaching some
sort of decision, for he abruptly took his foot down
from the railing. He stood for a moment, still looking
in Teddy's direction, then walked away, out of sight.
Not a minute later, though, he turned up, obtrusively
vertical, among the deck-chair ranks. He was about
thirty, or younger. He directly started to make his
way down-aisle toward Teddy's chair, casting distracting
little shadows over the pages of people's novels and
stepping rather uninhibitedly (considering that his was
the only standing, moving figure in sight) over knitting
bags and other personal effects.

Teddy seemed oblivious of the fact that someone
was standing at the foot of his chair—or, for that
matter, casting a shadow over his notebook. A few
people in the row or two behind him, however, were
more distractible. They looked up at the young man as,
perhaps, only people in deck chairs can look up at
someone. The young man had a kind of poise about
him, though, that looked as though it might hold up
indefinitely, with the very small proviso that he keep

at least one hand in one pocket. "Hello, there!" he said to Teddy.

Teddy looked up. "Hello," he said. He partly closed his notebook, partly let it close by itself.

"Mind if I sit down a minute?" the young man asked, with what seemed to be unlimited cordiality. "This anybody's chair?"

"Well, these four chairs belong to my family," Teddy said. "But my parents aren't up yet."

"Not *up?* On a day like this," the young man said. He had already lowered himself into the chair at Teddy's right. The chairs were placed so close together that the arms touched. "That's sacrilege," he said. "Absolute sacrilege." He stretched out his legs, which were unusually heavy at the thighs, almost like human bodies in themselves. He was dressed, for the most part, in Eastern seaboard regimentals: a turf haircut on top, run-down brogues on the bottom, with a somewhat mixed uniform in between—buff-colored woolen socks, charcoal-gray trousers, a button-down-collar shirt, no necktie, and a herringbone jacket that looked as though it had been properly aged in some of the more popular postgraduate seminars at Yale, or Harvard, or Princeton. "Oh, God, what a divine day," he said appreciatively, squinting up at the sun. "I'm an absolute pawn when it comes to the weather." He crossed his heavy legs, at the ankles. "As a matter of fact, I've been known to take a perfectly normal rainy day as a personal insult. So this is absolute manna to me." Though his speaking voice was, in the usual connotation, well bred, it carried considerably more than adequately, as though he had some sort of understanding with himself that anything he had to say would sound pretty much all right—intelligent, literate, even amusing or stimulating—either from Teddy's vantage point or from that of the people in the row behind, if they were listening. He looked obliquely down at Teddy, and smiled. "How are you and the weather?" he asked. His smile was not unpersonable, but it was social, or conversational, and related back, however indirectly, to his own ego. "The weather ever bother you out of all sensible proportion?" he asked, smiling.

"I don't take it too personal, if that's what you mean," Teddy said.

The young man laughed, letting his head go back. "Wonderful," he said. "My name, incidentally, is Bob Nicholson. I don't know if we quite got around to that in the gym. I know *your* name, of course."

Teddy shifted his weight over to one hip and stashed his notebook in the side pocket of his shorts.

"I was watching you write—from way up there," Nicholson said, narratively, pointing. "Good Lord. You were working away like a little Trojan."

Teddy looked at him. "I was writing something in my notebook."

Nicholson nodded, smiling. "How was Europe?" he asked conversationally. "Did you enjoy it?"

"Yes, very much, thank you."

"Where all did you go?"

Teddy suddenly reached forward and scratched the calf of his leg. "Well, it would take me too much time to name all the places, because we took our car and drove fairly great distances." He sat back. "My mother and I were mostly in Edinburgh, Scotland, and Oxford, England, though. I think I told you in the gym I had to be interviewed at both those places. Mostly the University of Edinburgh."

"No, I don't believe you did," Nicholson said. "I

was wondering if you'd done anything like that. How'd it go? They grill you?"

"I beg your pardon?" Teddy said.

"How'd it go? Was it interesting?"

"At times, yes. At times, no," Teddy said. "We stayed a little bit too long. My father wanted to get back to New York a little sooner than this ship. But some people were coming over from Stockholm, Sweden, and Innsbruck, Austria, to meet me, and we had to wait around."

"It's always that way."

Teddy looked at him directly for the first time. "Are you a poet?" he asked.

"A poet?" Nicholson said. "Lord, no. Alas, no. Why do you ask?"

"I don't know. Poets are always taking the weather so personally. They're always sticking their emotions in things that have no emotions."

Nicholson, smiling, reached into his jacket pocket and took out cigarettes and matches. "I rather thought that was their stock in trade," he said. "Aren't emotions what poets are primarily concerned with?"

Teddy apparently didn't hear him, or wasn't listening. He was looking abstractedly toward, or over, the twin smokestacks up on the Sports Deck.

Nicholson got his cigarette lit, with some difficulty, for there was a light breeze blowing from the north. He sat back, and said, "I understand you left a pretty disturbed bunch—"

" 'Nothing in the voice of the cicada intimates how soon it will die,' " Teddy said suddenly. " 'Along this road goes no one, this autumn eve.' "

"What was that?" Nicholson asked, smiling. "Say that again."

"Those are two Japanese poems. They're not full

of a lot of emotional stuff," Teddy said. He sat forward abruptly, tilted his head to the right, and gave his right ear a light clap with his hand. "I still have some water in my ear from my swimming lesson yesterday," he said. He gave his ear another couple of claps, then sat back, putting his arms up on both armrests. It was, of course, a normal, adult-size deck chair, and he looked distinctly small in it, but at the same time, he looked perfectly relaxed, even serene.

"I understand you left a pretty disturbed bunch of pedants up at Boston," Nicholson said, watching him. "After that last little set-to. The whole Leidekker examining group, more or less, the way I understand it. I believe I told you I had rather a long chat with Al Babcock last June. Same night, as a matter of fact, I heard your tape played off."

"Yes, you did. You told me."

"I understand they were a pretty disturbed bunch," Nicholson pressed. "From What Al told me, you all had quite a little lethal bull session late one night— the same night you made that tape, I believe." He took a drag on his cigarette. "From what I gather, you made some little predictions that disturbed the boys no end. Is that right?"

"I wish I knew why people think it's so important to be emotional," Teddy said. "My mother and father don't think a person's human unless he thinks a lot of things are very sad or very annoying or very—very un*just,* sort of. My father gets very emotional even when he reads the newspaper. He thinks I'm inhuman."

Nicholson flicked his cigarette ash off to one side. "I take it you have no emotions?" he said.

Teddy reflected before answering. "If I do, I don't remember when I ever used them," he said. "I don't see what they're *good* for."

"You love God, don't you?" Nicholson asked, with a little excess of quietness. "Isn't that your forte, so to speak? From what I heard on that tape and from what Al Babcock—"

"Yes, sure, I love Him. But I don't love Him sentimentally. He never said anybody had to love Him sentimentally," Teddy said. "If *I* were God, I certainly wouldn't want people to love me sentimentally. It's too unreliable."

"You love your parents, don't you?"

"Yes, I do—very much," Teddy said, "but you want to make me use that word to mean what you want it to mean—I can tell."

"All right. In what sense do *you* want to use it?"

Teddy thought it over. "You know what the word 'affinity' means?" he asked, turning to Nicholson.

"I have a rough idea," Nicholson said dryly.

"I have a very strong affinity for them. They're my parents, I mean, and we're all part of each other's harmony and everything," Teddy said. "I want them to have a nice time while they're alive, because they like having a nice time . . . But they don't love me and Booper—that's my sister—that way. I mean they don't seem able to love us just the way we are. They don't seem able to love us unless they can keep changing us a little bit. They love their reasons for loving us almost as much as they love us, and most of the time more. It's not so good, that way." He turned toward Nicholson again, sitting slightly forward. "Do you have the time, please?" he asked. "I have a swimming lesson at ten-thirty."

"You have time," Nicholson said without first looking at his wrist watch. He pushed back his cuff. "It's just ten after ten," he said.

"Thank you," Teddy said, and sat back. "We can

enjoy our conversation for about ten more minutes."

Nicholson let one leg drop over the side of the deck chair, leaned forward, and stepped on his cigarette end. "As I understand it," he said, sitting back, "you hold pretty firmly to the Vedantic theory of reincarnation."

"It isn't a theory, it's as much a part—"

"All right," Nicholson said quickly. He smiled, and gently raised the flats of his hands, in a sort of ironic benediction. "We won't argue that point, for the moment. Let me finish." He crossed his heavy, outstretched legs again. "From what I gather, you've acquired certain information, through meditation, that's given you some conviction that in your last incarnation you were a holy man in India, but more or less fell from Grace—"

"I wasn't a holy man," Teddy said. "I was just a person making very nice spiritual advancement."

"All right—whatever it was," Nicholson said. "But the point is you feel that in your last incarnation you more or less fell from Grace before final Illumination. Is that right, or am I—"

"That's right," Teddy said. "I met a lady, and I sort of stopped meditating." He took his arms down from the armrests, and tucked his hands, as if to keep them warm, under his thighs. "I would have had to take another body and come back to earth again *any*way—I mean I wasn't so spiritually advanced that I could have died, if I hadn't met that lady, and then gone straight to Brahma and never again have to come back to earth. But I wouldn't have had to get incarnated in an American body if I hadn't met that lady. I mean it's very hard to meditate and live a spiritual life in America. People think you're a freak if you try to. My father thinks I'm a freak, in a way.

And my mother—well, she doesn't think it's good for me to think about God all the time. She thinks it's bad for my health."

Nicholson was looking at him, studying him. "I believe you said on that last tape that you were six when you first had a mystical experience. Is that right?"

"I was six when I saw that everything was God, and my hair stood up, and all that," Teddy said. "It was on a Sunday, I remember. My sister was only a very tiny child then, and she was drinking her milk, and all of a sudden I saw that *she* was God and the *milk* was God. I mean, all she was doing was pouring God into God, if you know what I mean."

Nicholson didn't say anything.

"But I could get out of the finite dimensions fairly often when I was four," Teddy said, as an afterthought. "Not continuously or anything, but fairly often."

Nicholson nodded. "You did?" he said. "You could?"

"Yes," Teddy said. "That was on the tape . . . Or maybe it was on the one I made last April. I'm not sure."

Nicholson took out his cigarettes again, but without taking his eyes off Teddy. "How does one get out of the finite dimensions?" he asked, and gave a short laugh. "I mean, to begin very basically, a block of wood is a block of wood, for example. It has length, width—"

"It hasn't. That's where you're wrong," Teddy said. "Everybody just *thinks* things keep stopping off somewhere. They don't. That's what I was trying to tell Professor Peet." He shifted in his seat and took out an eyesore of a handkerchief—a gray, wadded entity—and blew his nose. "The reason things *seem* to stop off somewhere is because that's the only way most people know how to look at things," he said. "But that doesn't mean they do." He put away his handkerchief, and looked at Nicholson. "Would you hold up your arm a second, please?" he asked.

"My arm? Why?"

"Just do it. Just do it a second."

Nicholson raised his forearm an inch or two above the level of the armrest. "This one?" he asked.

Teddy nodded. "What do you call that?" he asked.

"What do you mean? It's my arm. It's an *arm*."

"How do you know it is?" Teddy asked. "You know it's called an arm, but how do you know it is one? Do you have any proof that it's an arm?"

Nicholson took a cigarette out of his pack, and lit it. "I think that smacks of the worst kind of sophistry, frankly," he said, exhaling smoke. "It's an arm, for heaven's sake, because it's an arm. In the first place, it has to have a name to distinguish it from other objects. I mean you can't simply—"

"You're just being logical," Teddy said to him impassively.

"I'm just being what?" Nicholson asked, with a little excess of politeness.

"Logical. You're just giving me a regular, intelligent answer," Teddy said. "I was trying to help you. You asked me how I get out of the finite dimensions when I feel like it. I certainly don't use logic when I do it. Logic's the first thing you have to get rid of."

Nicholson removed a flake of tobacco from his tongue with his fingers.

"You know Adam?" Teddy asked him.

"Do I know who?"

"Adam. In the Bible."

Nicholson smiled. "Not personally," he said dryly.

Teddy hesitated. "Don't be angry with me," he said. "You asked me a question, and I'm—"

"I'm not *angry* with you, for heaven's sake."

"Okay," Teddy said. He was sitting back in his chair, but his head was turned toward Nicholson. "You know that apple Adam ate in the Garden of Eden, referred to in the Bible?" he asked. "You know what was in that apple? Logic. Logic and intellectual stuff. That was all that was in it. So—this is my point— what you have to do is vomit it up if you want to see things as they really are. I mean if you vomit it up, then you won't have any more trouble with blocks of wood and stuff. You won't see everything stopping *off* all the time. And you'll know what your arm really is, if you're interested. Do you know what I mean? Do you follow me?"

"I follow you," Nicholson said, rather shortly.

"The trouble is," Teddy said, "most people don't want to see things the way they are. They don't even want to stop getting born and dying all the time. They just want new bodies all the time, instead of stopping and staying with God, where it's really nice." He reflected. "I never saw such a bunch of apple-eaters," he said. He shook his head.

At that moment, a white-coated deck steward, who was making his rounds within the area, stopped in front of Teddy and Nicholson and asked them if they would care to have morning broth. Nicholson didn't respond to the question at all. Teddy said, "No, thank you," and the deck steward passed them by.

"If you'd rather not discuss this, you don't have to," Nicholson said abruptly, and rather brusquely. He flicked his cigarette ash. "But is it true, or isn't

it, that you informed the whole Leidekker examining
bunch—Walton, Peet, Larsen, Samuels, and that
bunch—when and where and how they would eventually die? Is that true, or isn't it? You don't have to
discuss it if you don't want to, but the way the rumor
around Boston—"

"No, it is not true," Teddy said with emphasis. "I
told them places, and *times,* when they should be very,
very careful. And I told them certain things it might
be a good idea for them to *do* . . . But I didn't say
anything like *that.* I didn't say anything was inevitable,
that way." He took out his handkerchief again and
used it. Nicholson waited, watching him. "And I didn't
tell Professor Peet anything like that at all. Firstly, he
wasn't one of the ones who were kidding around and
asking me a bunch of questions. I mean all I told
Professor Peet was that he shouldn't be a teacher any
more after January—that's all I told him." Teddy, sitting back, was silent a moment. "All those other
professors, they practically forced me to tell them all
that stuff. It was after we were all finished with the in-
terview and making that tape, and it was quite late,
and they all kept sitting around smoking cigarettes and
getting very kittenish."

"But you didn't tell Walton, or Larsen, for example,
when or where or how death would eventually come?"
Nicholson pressed.

"*No.* I did not," Teddy said firmly. "I wouldn't have
told them *any* of that stuff, but they kept *talk*ing
about it. Professor Walton sort of started it. He said
he really wished he knew when he was going to die,
because then he'd know what work he should do and
what work he shouldn't do, and how to use his time
to his best advantage, and all like that. And then they
all said that . . . So I told them a little bit."

Nicholson didn't say anything.

"I didn't tell them when they were actually going to die, though. That's a very false rumor," Teddy said. "I *could* have, but I knew that in their hearts they really didn't want to know. I mean I knew that even though they teach Religion and Philosophy and all, they're still pretty afraid to die." Teddy sat, or reclined, in silence for a minute. "It's so silly," he said. "All you do is get the heck out of your body when you die. My gosh, everybody's done it thousands and thousands of times. Just because they don't remember it doesn't mean they haven't done it. It's so silly."

"That may be. That may be," Nicholson said. "But the logical fact remains that no matter how intelligently—"

"It's so silly," Teddy said again. "For example, I have a swimming lesson in about five minutes. I could go downstairs to the pool, and there might not be any water in it. This might be the day they change the water or something. What might happen, though, I might walk up to the edge of it, just to have a look at the bottom, for instance, and my sister might come up and sort of push me in. I could fracture my skull and die instantaneously." Teddy looked at Nicholson. "That could happen," he said. "My sister's only six, and she hasn't been a human being for very many lives, and she doesn't like me very much. That could happen, all right. What would be so tragic about it, though? What's there to be afraid of, I mean? I'd just be doing what I was supposed to do, that's all, wouldn't I?"

Nicholson snorted mildly. "It might not be a tragedy from your point of view, but it would certainly be a sad event for your mother and dad," he said. "Ever consider that?"

"Yes, of course, I have," Teddy said. "But that's only because they have names and emotions for everything that happens." He had been keeping his hands tucked under his legs again. He took them out now, put his arms up on the armrests, and looked at Nicholson. "You know Sven? The man that takes care of the gym?" he asked. He waited till he got a nod from Nicholson. "Well, if Sven dreamed tonight that his dog died, he'd have a very, very bad night's sleep, because he's very fond of that dog. But when he woke up in the morning, everything would be all right. He'd know it was only a dream."

Nicholson nodded. "What's the point, exactly?"

"The point is if his dog really died, it would be exactly the same thing. Only, he wouldn't know it. I mean he wouldn't wake up till he died himself."

Nicholson, looking detached, was using his right hand to give himself a slow, sensuous massage at the back of the neck. His left hand, motionless on the armrest, with a fresh, unlighted cigarette between the fingers, looked oddly white and inorganic in the brilliant sunlight.

Teddy suddenly got up. "I really have to go now, I'm afraid," he said. He sat down, tentatively, on the extended leg attachment of his chair, facing Nicholson, and tucked in his T shirt. "I have about one and a half minutes, I guess, to get to my swimming lesson," he said. "It's all the way down on E Deck."

"May I ask why you told Professor Peet he should stop teaching after the first of the year?" Nicholson asked, rather bluntly. "I know Bob Peet. That's why I ask."

Teddy tightened his alligator belt. "Only because he's quite spiritual, and he's teaching a lot of stuff right now that isn't very good for him if he wants to make any real spiritual advancement. It stimulates him too much. It's time for him to take everything *out* of his head, instead of putting more stuff *in*. He could get rid of a lot of the apple in just this one life if he wanted to. He's very good at meditating." Teddy got up. "I better go now. I don't want to be too late."

Nicholson looked up at him, and sustained the look —detaining him. "What would you do if you could change the educational system?" he asked ambiguously. "Ever think about that at all?"

"I really have to go," Teddy said.

"Just answer that one question," Nicholson said. "Education's my baby, actually—that's what I teach. That's why I ask."

"Well . . . I'm not too sure what I'd do," Teddy said. "I know I'm pretty sure I wouldn't start with the things schools usually start with." He folded his arms, and reflected briefly. "I think I'd first just assemble all the children together and show them how to meditate. I'd try to show them how to find out who they *are,* not just what their names are and things like that . . . I guess, even before that, I'd get them to empty out everything their parents and everybody ever told them. I mean even if their parents just told them an elephant's big, I'd make them empty *that* out. An elephant's only big when it's next to something else—a dog or a lady, for example." Teddy thought another moment. "I wouldn't even tell them an elephant has a trunk. I might *show* them an elephant, if I had one handy, but I'd let them just walk up to the elephant not knowing anything more about it than the elephant knew about *them.* The same thing with grass, and other things. I wouldn't even tell them grass is green. Colors are only names. I mean if you tell them the grass is green, it makes them start expecting the grass to look a certain way—*your* way—instead of some other way that may be just as good, and maybe much better . . . I don't know. I'd just make them vomit up every bit of the apple their parents and everybody made them take a bite out of."

"There's no risk you'd be raising a little generation of ignoramuses?"

"Why? They wouldn't any more be ignoramuses than an elephant is. Or a bird is. Or a tree is," Teddy said. "Just because something *is* a certain way, instead of just behaves a certain way, doesn't mean it's an ignoramus."

"No?"

"No!" Teddy said. "Besides, if they wanted to learn all that other stuff—names and colors and things—they could do it, if they felt like it, later on when they were older. But I'd want them to *begin* with all the real ways of looking at things, not just the way all the other apple-eaters look at things—that's what I mean." He came closer to Nicholson, and extended his hand down to him. "I have to go now. Honestly. I've enjoyed—"

"Just one second—sit down a minute," Nicholson said. "Ever think you might like to do something in research when you grow up? Medical research, or something of that kind? It seems to me, with your mind, you might eventually—"

Teddy answered, but without sitting down. "I thought about that once, a couple of years ago," he said. "I've talked to quite a few doctors." He shook his head. "That wouldn't interest me very much. Doctors stay too right on the surface. They're always talking about cells and things."

"Oh? You don't attach any importance to cell structure?"

"Yes, sure, I do. But doctors talk about cells as if they had such unlimited importance all by themselves. As if they didn't really belong to the person that has them." Teddy brushed back his hair from his forehead with one hand. "I grew my own body," he said. "Nobody else did it for me. So if I grew it, I must have known *how* to grow it. Unconsciously, at least. I may have lost the *con*scious knowledge of how to grow it sometime in the last few hundred thousand years, but the knowledge is still *there,* because—obviously—I've used it. . . . It would take quite a lot of meditation and emptying out to get the whole thing back—I mean the conscious knowledge—but you could do it if you wanted to. If you opened up wide enough." He suddenly reached down and picked up Nicholson's right hand from the armrest. He shook it just once, cordially, and said, "Goodbye. I have to go." And this time, Nicholson wasn't able to detain him, he started so quickly to make his way through the aisle.

Nicholson sat motionless for some few minutes after he left, his hands on the armrests of the chair, his unlighted cigarette still between the fingers of his left hand. Finally, he raised his right hand and used it as if to check whether his collar was still open. Then he lit his cigarette, and sat quite still again.

He smoked the cigarette down to its end, then abruptly let one foot over the side of the chair, stepped on the cigarette, got to his feet, and made his way, rather quickly, out of the aisle.

Using the forwardship stairway, he descended fairly briskly to the Promenade Deck. Without stopping there, he continued on down, still quite rapidly, to Main Deck. Then to A Deck. Then to B Deck. Then to C Deck. Then to D Deck.

At D Deck the forwardship stairway ended, and Nicholson stood for a moment, apparently at some loss for direction. However, he spotted someone who looked able to guide him. Halfway down the passageway, a stewardess was sitting on a chair outside a galleyway, reading a magazine and smoking a cigarette. Nicholson went down to her, consulted her briefly, thanked her, then took a few additional steps forwardship and opened a heavy metal door that read: TO THE POOL. It opened onto a narrow, uncarpeted staircase.

He was little more than halfway down the staircase when he heard an all-piercing, sustained scream —clearly coming from a small, female child. It was highly acoustical, as though it were reverberating within four tiled walls.